Risen

The Battle for Darracia (Book III)

Michael Phillip Cash

Copyright © 2014 Michael Phillip Cash

Published in the United States by

Red Feather Publishing

New York—Los Angeles—Las Vegas

All rights reserved.

ISBN-13: 9781499242676
ISBN-10: 1499242670

Disclaimer

The characters and events portrayed in this book are fictitious. Any resemblance to real persons, living or dead, on Earth or on Darracia, is coincidental and not intended by the author.

No part of this book may be reproduced, stored in a retrieval system, or transmitted in any form or by any means—electronic, mechanical, photocopying, recording, or otherwise—without express written permission of the publisher.

Dedication

To Kevin

"I am thankful that in a troubled world no calamity can prevent the return of spring."—Helen Keller

Follow Darracia
@michaelpcash

www.michaelphillipcash.com

If you find this book enjoyable, I really hope you'll leave a review on Amazon, Goodreads, or Barnes & Noble under *Risen: The Battle for Darracia, Book 3*. If you have any questions or comments, please contact me directly at **michaelphillipcash@gmail.com**.

Praise for Michael Phillip Cash's debut book, *Brood X: A Firsthand Account of the Great Cicada Invasion*

- Simple, straightforward, flashlight-on-the-face campfire tale meant to induce nightmares."—***Mark McLaughlin, ForeWord Reviews***

- "Cash has written a harrowing tale of survival against all odds of a supernatural nature. As summer gets hot, *Brood X* will cool you down by sending chills down your back."—***Nina Schuyler, Author, The Translator***

- "Part creature-feature with all of the traditional elements of the great '50s films…part homage to the fairly recent genre of found-footage horror films—*Brood X* is a quick, fun read."—***Michael R. Collings, hellnotes.com***

- "A *Twilight Zone*–like horror story of biblical proportions."—***Mark McLaughlin, ForeWord Reviews***

- "Horror at its best…up close and personal and inflicted with ways that address humanity's inherent fear of and disgust for bugs."—***Mark McLaughlin, ForeWord Reviews***

- "Breathing new life into a genre that has been occupied too long by the usual suspects: sickness, the undead, and global warming."—***Kirkus Review***

Critics love Cash's paranormal romance novel, *Stillwell: A Haunting on Long Island*

- "Cash easily draws readers into the story by creating three-dimensional characters who are easy to care about…Thriller meets love story in a novel where characterization shines…with strong characters and a twist unexpected in a thriller, this book is an enjoyable beach read."—***ForeWord Reviews***

- "Michael Phillip Cash is creating a niche in the pantheon of successful young writers of the day."—***Grady Harp, Amazon Top Reviewer***

- "*Stillwell* has all the gothic-type elements of the old great books with some of the new and satisfying elements that make it very readable and enjoyable."—***The Gothic Wanderer***

- "A great read! Mr. Cash, I foresee more fast-paced thrillers in your future. A well-written story with engaging characters."—***MyBookAddiction Reviews***

- "*Stillwell* is a book that will keep you on the edge of your seat all the way through…it is one of the best books I have read in years."—***Chronicles from a Caveman***

- "A horror tale with well-developed characters…" —***Kirkus Review***

- "I do not see what would stop Michael Phillip Cash's horror masterpiece from becoming a best-seller."—***pjtheemt.blogspot.com***

rīz/en

verb
1. to get up after falling or being thrown down

"The greater the obstacle, the more glory in overcoming it."

– **Molière**

Book Three

Chapter 1

V'sair became aware of a cushion supporting him first. He was weightless, his mind in the hazy netherworld between lilac-colored dreams and sepia reality. His arms rose, as if supported by marionette's strings. He was wet but didn't notice it. He saw the dull sheen of the bars of the cage imprisoning him but couldn't seem to care. Eyes sliding shut, the siren of sleep called him, the air escaped from his body in a long hiss. Sounds mutated to become soft music, and he relaxed drifting in peaceful solitude. Closing his eyes, he let go of life, allowing a final stream of bubbles to escape his lax lips. He floated in an abyss, his senses dulled, his mind lethargic. His skin pebbled as the water grew colder, wrapping a vice around his chest. His body numb, his legs heavy, he spiraled downward, enveloped by lassitude. With detached calm, he observed two burly males, their skin tinted an opalescent blue a bit lighter than his own, using their combined strength to pull the golden bars apart. They were trying to get to him, he thought indifferently, watching as if he were a spectator in some drama. The water swirled, buffeting him gently as it was stirred by a being next to him. A female swam close to him, he felt her cool hands grab his chin. Lips covered his—a soft kiss, blowing gently, his nostrils flaring in indignation at the interruption. His eyes opened wide to see her face close to his, fine green hair creating a swirling cocoon, wrapping around his chilled body. The tendrils caressed his skin, warming him, awakening him in a sensual dance. V'sair arched painfully as his skin tore, five gills ripping into each of his sides to undulate, forcing seawater into his starved lungs. His chest expanded, salty fluid invading his lungs. His body filled, choking him, making him gag. Rolling violently, he struggled like a hooked trout, only to feel iron hands pull him through the small opening, abrading his sensitive skin against the rough metal, then steadying him in a vice-like embrace. Both his arms and legs were straightened by another pair of hands. V'sair kicked back wildly. A scream rose to explode from his throat in a giant silver bubble that escaped, rising before him like liquid mercury. Firm fingers grabbed his thrashing head, holding it still, until he exhausted himself. The hands held him, until his eyes opened to find a light blue face with huge, clear eyes studying him.

She was distinctly female. Four large males surrounded him, holding his weak body. The girl's small mouth opened as she communicated, but all V'sair heard was garbled clicks, followed by a whine, not unlike the string instruments played in his court. She was almost a comical creature, with two holes where the nose should be, a high, intelligent forehead, and those unearthly clear eyes that studied him intently. A web hand slapped his face, the water cushioning the blow, but it did get his attention. She resembled his mother slightly. Reminda had more defined features—a larger nose and, of course, her beautiful, orange facial tattoos. He looked wildly around, taking in the five creatures. They were all kicking easily, while he worked hard to float. Certainly he saw differences from his Plantan ancestors, but where did they come from? He watched the blue-tinged face with bulbous eyes, swimming gracefully before him. She studied him intently. He saw her irises were a light blue; they were not clear at all. The sounds came to him and occurred to his dazed brain that she was speaking to him. He forced himself to concentrate, but the lack of air muddied his mind. He realized with a start that he was indeed breathing, water trickling in through his chest to be expelled though his lips. Scrambling, he ripped at his shirt, and the female brushed his hands away to help him lift the garment. V'sair's eyes widened at tiny, raw gills working hard on each side of his chest. He was familiar with gills; his mother had them. He touched the top one. The sensitive flesh trembled when, as he ran the pad of his fingertip, his mouth opened in shock as well as awe. It appeared as though he had been surgically cut, but he knew that was not true. They were tender. His whole body was sore. Tiny bubbles escaped. He looked up to see the creature smile with a nod. He depressed the gill, feeling himself choke as though he was being smothered. The female spoke again, but he shook his head. He didn't understand her. She pulled his hand away, slapping his wrist light, then shook her finger at him. Clearly, he was being told to leave his newly formed gills alone.

She swam around him, her body long, her webfeet so like his mother's. She was young, perhaps his own age, maybe younger. V'sair stared at her, a feeling a familiarity nagging at his brain. He shook his head as if to clear his fogged head. The female took his hand coming alongside of him horizontally, then hooked his fingertips to urge him to follow. He barrel rolled, unused to the currents of water streaming around them. Two of the males steadied him and, with a nod, showed him the direction they would be swimming. They made no eye contact with him but took their commands from the girl. Her hair floated around her like seaweed, shrimp and other small creatures nesting in its glorious depths. He reached out to take a small urchin, staring with wonder, but the girl plucked it from his fingers, letting it scuttle away on a wall of multicolored coral. V'sair turned to consider his surroundings. He was well and truly deep in the Hixom Sea, either dead or learning how to use his inborn skill to breathe underwater. Fluid burned in his nose, his eyes winced, and he looked up to find her laughing at his discomfort. He realized he was instinctively scissoring his legs, the motion keeping his floating feet off the murky ocean floor. His eyes adjusted to the darkness, and he glanced around, taking in rainbow-hued coral, teeming with tiny creatures in a multitude of pastel shades. The water had settled, and the sand was a pale pink, littered with orange starfish. He bent to pick one up and was snatched backward by one of the burly males swimming next to him. The girl shook her finger with admonishment. She swam downward, reaching for a long branch of coral discarded on the floor. She tapped the starfish, which reared inward, revealing a circular mouth filled with snapping teeth. It snatched the coral from her hands, crushing it in its tiny jaws, reducing it to pink dust. The girl motioned for him to follow, and he realized with a start she was naked, save a small covering on her loins, not unlike the red seaweed that washed up on the shores of the beach. Clumsily, he surged forward, his movements awkward, with the gentle help of the four males surrounding him. They swam for hours, it seemed. V'sair's heart beat tiredly in his chest; his arms moved with leaden determination. Though he breathed the seawater, it irritated his chest, and he felt the need to cough every so often, pausing to hack uselessly.

He heard nothing except for his own pulse, beating wildly in his head—a steady tattoo that became a song of survival. By all rights, he should have been dead, and worry for his mother, Tulani, and his home weighed heavily in his chest. He paused to glance up at the distant surface. Crouching, he made to surge upward but was caught easily by one of the guards. V'sair struggled in the tight grip, fighting a losing battle. Taking a woven strand of some sort of hemp, one of the men tied it to his waist, imprisoning V'sair. Wearily, he stared at the smudged light just over the surface of the water, but the tug of the tether held him fast, propelling him swiftly along the ocean floor.

He glanced at his saviors. They were mythical creatures, he laughed to himself, spotted only by drunken Darracians. There were stories about beasts that swam deep in the sea, but no evidence had ever been found. For years, he had been teased about his resemblance to the legendary beings. Nobody really believed they existed. The likeness was nothing short of astonishing. V'sair paddled his feet furiously to keep up with the group. Every so often, he slowed enough to be dragged along while he caught his breath. Breathing was hard, and his legs burned. Several times his eyes drifted shut with exhaustion, but still they traveled along the rugged ocean floor. It was a cornucopia of life forms, multihued creatures he could never imagine. Strange, long eels, yellow and black with neon green eyes. Giant clamshells rippled the water as they opened, revealing purple-flesh tongues that reached out to ensnare hard-shelled lobsters, daring to climb the scalloped-shaped shells. He saw schools of large fish, with tufts of brown hair that surrounded their pointed faces like old monkeys. His group froze, one of the male swimmers protectively pulling the female next to him.

His tired mind registered they were armed with long spears, with deadly sickle-shaped blades mounted on the top. A huge, gray-colored beast with a white belly lumbered by. Its skin sparkled like mica as it moved in the darkness of the water. He could see the frightened faces of the group. They barely breathed, and he held his breath as well. He was dragged behind a wall of gently swaying fronds, camouflaging them from the giant predator. It had an enormous maw for a mouth, a pointed snout with two pulsing nostrils, large enough to put his fist inside. A platter-sized eye, its black pupil took up the whole mass, turned its dead stare on them.

The female froze, her hand gripping the young king's forearm, holding him still. The monster opened its mouth revealing rows and rows of razor teeth the size of his forearm. They gleamed in the murky depths, small fish swimming innocently around the white sentinels as though it was a form of coral. The beast sniffed, the eyes rolled back turning white. One of the guards slowly raised his spear, aiming for the great eye, his bulging muscles quivering with intensity. The fish thrashed its tail, creating a tsunami of small waves, turning its great head to swim on in indifference to the tasty morsels it had just passed up.

The girls smiled, her small mouth exposing pointed white teeth. She said something to V'sair, and while he didn't understand her language, he comprehended she wanted him to hurry.

They swam down a ravine, the water becoming denser, the currents colder. V'sair couldn't stop the shivers running down his body. His legs cramped, paralyzing him, forcing him to curl into a tiny ball. Impatient hands grabbed him underneath his armpits, and he allowed them to take over, his body too tired to try. His head sagged, his chin resting on his chest, until they rounded the last hill to swim into a clearing with a large underwater volcano. V'sair forced himself to look, swallowing seawater that sent him into a coughing fit, snapping the last thread to his new reality. His last sight was of a vast underwater city, peopled by a busy population of this fish species.

Chapter 2

"He smells!" Cosfar said with disgust. "He smells, and his odor will give us away to the Plantans."

The handsome Quyroo walked next to Bobbien, his fist in the air. He was the de facto leader in the bush, taking control when Lothen and the Plantan ship bombed their homes.

"I say we give him up to the Plantans, trade him for some of ours." He wheedled. He was tall, with an imposing air of leadership. He ran a hand through the tangle of his braids leaving them disordered, making him lose his look of authority.

Bobbien chuckled, then shook her staff at him, the dried gourds at the top making a rattling noise. "Enough, Cosfar. He is injured. He needs time to heal."

"He is Darracian. Let him heal with his own kind," the Quyroo spat, his braids shaking as he shook his head in anger. He was tall and liked to use his superior height to intimidate the older woman.

"Throw him in prison, they will," Bobbien responded, brushing his concerns away with her hand.

"Who cares? They did nothing for us when the Plantans destroyed the Desa." Cosfar followed her, leaning too close when he spoke. She stopped, using her staff to create boundary of personal space between them. He was popular; Bobbien just didn't know why. He did have a winning way with the elders, as well as the young females. Bobbien didn't trust him or his sleazy ways. All he did was criticize her for speaking in the archaic ways of their ancestors. Bobbien did try to modernize her speech patterns but found herself slipping into Oldspeak, and became the butt of Cosfar's jokes. He was always taking credit for things. When she ran the risk of finding food supplies, he claimed it was he who found it. He challenged everything she suggested, making creation of any rules to bring order to the growing encampment impossible. The group had grown, spreading under the last of the great Desa to hide from the invaders. She found herself too often squaring off with him. Whether it was regarding medicine, sanitation, or dispensing of food, it seems all they did was lock heads with each other. She had known his parents and remembered thinking he was a petulant child when he was young.

Bobbien thought before answering him. Anything she told him would be spread in the camps later. "Unprepared they were." She looked at him hard and stressed. "They have never been attacked with cannon before."
"Look you, Bobbien." Cosfar pointed to Syos, the red rock city in the clouds. "Their home survives. Life goes on for the Darracian." He pounded his chest indignantly. "Only the Quyroo homes were destroyed. Life is as it was for them."

"Not quite, Cosfar," Bobbien interrupted him. "See the city." She pointed her long, red arm upward.

It was clear things has changed. The city in the clouds no longer teemed with Darracians. Syos was deserted, the fine red walls of the city pockmarked and dull from the attack. There was a seedy air of decay about the buildings. Repairs had never been made; it seems Plantans only understood destruction. Few patrols dotted the sky. She could tell their resources were strapped. The Plantan population was aggressive but small. Yet they managed a total takeover by breaking the back of many of the noble houses. Lothen understood that he had to divide and conquer, and that is exactly what he did. Tree dwellers fell back into the forests with the ground dwellers. Former enemies became allies. Darracian were alone with the intruders. The people of the earth were not wanted in the new society. They were disappearing. It was as though the population in the Desa had never existed. Bobbien's eyes narrowed as she stared at the defeated city. It hovered closer to the planet, the Randam crystals used as a power source to keep it floating, running low. Many of the valuable trees were destroyed in the invasion, leaving the crystals to decay. There was a limited work force trying to harvest them. It was a skill only known by the Quyroos, and the stupid Plantans eliminated the hunters. The lights dimmed on the city towers and walls, leaving a fuzzy outline of where once stood a beautiful civilization.

"Now they have total control of the Randam crystals, and we are left to molder in the swamp. They are making slaves of our people. I have heard of transports." Cosfar stated angrily.

"Transports?" Bobbien asked.

"Any Quyroos captured are being transported out to only Sradda knows where."

"Most of those left are hiding in the Eastern Provinces. Find us, they won't." She shrugged, letting him know the conversation was finished.

Cosfar nodded. "That is true," he conceded. "How long do you think before they figure out how to get through the quicksand to get to us."

She turned patiently to explain it to him slowly, as though he were a dull-witted child.
"Travel through the Eastern Fells, they won't. The rain has made it impossible."

"But Bobbien," Cosfar continued. "Not even the Wysbies will stop them. They don't like Plantan blood. The time of rains has taken out all natural predators. The herns have become extinct. They have murdered them all."

"Given time, extinct the Plantans will be." Bobbien smiled, though in her heart all she cared about was Tulani. She hadn't heard from her granddaughter since V'sair was thrown into the Hixom Sea. She had traveled to Plains of Dawid, disguised in voluminous robes, and visited the new marketplace set up by that bully Seren but could find no information about the girl. It was a raw place with its lack of regulations, coupled with rampant shortages that made prices skyrocket. Food was at a premium. Medicines, other vital goods were becoming scarce, and a valuable trading commody. Stalls were set up, mostly by displaced Darracians, the Quyroo population inexplicably getting thinner and thinner. The Quyroo were disappearing and not all to the Eastern Provinces. The new town was rife with rumors, but sources were unreliable. Bobbien was a concrete kind of person. Until she saw it with her own eyes, she didn't accept anything she heard. But not finding Tulani weighed heavily on her heart. She had to get Zayden moving. He was their last hope.

"Meanwhile, the problem of this big Darracian is on my shoulders, Bobbien. He is a nuisance." Cosfar began his nagging again.

Bobbien wanted to argue but knew she this was an argument she would lose.

They both turned to observe Zayden propped up against a tree, his hair a matted tangle in his face, several bottles of Roothes, the homemade alcohol of the Quyroos, discarded around him. He was filthy with muddied clothes and dirty face. He did smell. He was unwashed, unkempt and so drunk he couldn't even sit upright. Singing a foul song, he raised his unshaven face to the wet sky, letting his voice carry to the outer reaches of the camp, disturbing everyone's peace.

After the Plantans attacked, every Quyroo took to the treetops to escape deep into the red forests of the Desa. The bombs had rained down on them, indiscriminately hitting homes, hospitals, and schools, killing a large part of the population. Bobbien had set up a base camp deep in the swamps, where no Darracian had ever traveled. It was cold there, the dual rays of the suns prevented from warming the land by the overgrown tropical trees. The ground was a red, soupy mess, filled with snakes, rodents, and nasty predators that attacked without warning. It was not a safe place. No one ventured there, but the Quyroos knew it was their only salvation. It was unmapped, unexplored, and barely reachable. The population had been sorely compromised, but every day new groups found their way in. Some were wounded, many burned and close to death. Bobbien had her hands full. She worked hard to heal as many as she could, appealing to Ozre to help her do what she was trained to do.

Bobbien turned to see Cosfar's flinty gaze watching Denita intently. He rubbed his hands together with a laugh.

"What does she see in him, I ask you?" he demanded.

Bobbien shrugged. "Who understands other species? Loves him, she does."

"Loves him, she does." Cosfar sneered. "Can't you speak more modern? That is why they don't respect you. Anyway, Zayden is just half a man."

"Indeed Cosfar, but it is the important half that counts!" Bobbien laughed at his reddening face, ignoring his barbs. "Sometimes, my friend, half is enough."

"This conversation is not finished, Bobbien." Cosfar had lost patience.

"It's done when I say it done!" Bobbien retorted.

Cosfar snapped his jaw shut, grinding his teeth. He stalked off in the direction of the new office he had created for himself.

"Rude bastard," Bobbien thought with distaste. She better get Zayden on his feet. That power-hungry Quyroo was trouble, she knew. She smelled a lot more than Zayden's dirty laundry in the air. A storm much larger than their blasted weather was brewing. She considered the hulking Darracian. She had insisted he stay under the great janjan tree, the dripping leaves creating a noisy umbrella against the weather. She heard the message. When would he realize the Elements were trying to contact him? It was there, right in front of him, all around him, but he might as well have been deaf too. When was he going to realize the pattern, she wondered.

She had no time for Zayden and his pity. He would not see again; that she knew for sure. The girl who crashed landed with him had coddled him, and that was a problem too. The High Priestess barely had enough time to eat with all the sick and wounded. Zayden came far down on her list.

Oh, he was very ill in the beginning! She bathed his eye with Caylet tea. The Hallis tree was deep in the Desa, and she risked much to gather the leaves. Twice she was almost caught, but she liked him. He was at heart a good person and had great potential. If she was ever going to see her granddaughter again, she had to make him realize his capabilities. Bobbien knew leadership was in his blood. He alone could rally the Quyroos to repel the invasion. It was his birthright. While Cosfar had his bullying ways, she understood that he was not a born leader. He would crumble like melted sugar when challenged. Bobbien knew his type.

"Ozre, Ereth, Ine," she appealed silently. "Tired these old bones are getting. Great Sradda willing, make the man better. Make him see what the rain is doing. I am weary."

Silence answered her, and Bobbien realized if Zayden were to recover, it was up to them both to make it happen. A crowd of children had gathered around him, a group of young boys, four or five of them, threw leaves at the drunken man. They giggled as he blindly waved his flailing hands. One of them picked up a rock, and Bobbien started purposefully toward him. She noticed Zayden had cocked his head in her direction, a small clicking sound reaching her ears. Bobbien smiled.

Zayden chose that moment to let loose a great belch, followed by lyrics so foul the crowd dispersed—mothers covering the ears of the young. Bobbien shrugged, and her face colored with embarrassment. But she knew she had to get this great, lumbering Darracian sober again, or she would lose all her newfound credibility. Still, she did hear the clicks. Perhaps the janjan tree had done its work. Standing in lee side of a broken trunk, she picked up a handful of pebbles. Using her thumb, she flicked them to land nearby. He was oblivious at first, but then she noticed a shift. His back grew rigid, and he appeared to sit up straighter, his head cocked as if he was suddenly aware of the noise. "Yes, yes," she thought, throwing the pebbles around his form. She watched his great head follow the movement. The rain changed to a downpour, and she smiled, knowing the leafy fronds would be pitter-pattering all around him. Standing taller, she winced at the cracking in her knees, kneading the chink in her back. "Elements! Take over for me, huh?" She laughed.

She walked through the crowds of Quyroo sitting on the ground toward the hut she shared with the Venturian female. The female was loyal to Zayden; Bobbien would give her that. Most girls would have run in the opposite direction saddled with a drunken cripple. Denita was on her knees, reaching under a cot to grab a bunch of roots and vegetables that Zayden had kicked around earlier. Bobbien bent to help her. Denita herself had just gotten over a bout of hufen. She had been one of the first cases, her stomach rejecting any food. Bobbien worried for the girl, who had no immunity to this planet's diseases, but she survived. Denita hid her illness from Zayden, sitting as quiet as a ghost in the hut so he wouldn't think her sick. So absorbed in his own troubles, Zayden remained remote. Bobbien wanted to shake him senseless.

"I would make him retrieve them," Bobbien told Denita as she crouched down to help.

Denita paused to give her a sideways look. "He didn't mean to; he is tired of this kind of food. Darracians eat meat."

"Spoil him, you do, Denita. He's never going to get better if you don't make him help himself."

"Easy for you to say. How am I supposed to make him see again?" Denita asked angrily.

"Believe in the Elements, do you?" Bobbien asked softly.

"There are no Elements on Venturian." The girl shrugged indifferently. She held a fruit in her palm, squeezing it gently. Bobbien laid a long-fingered red hand on top of the girl's.

"Everywhere are the Elements," Bobbien told her, holding her arms outstretched.

"If they are everywhere, how could they let a man like Zayden be blinded? How could they leave your granddaughter a prisoner, or worse, perhaps?"

"Aye, it looks grim, but…" Bobbien stood to go to the crude window to look out on their small camp. "There is a reason for all this. The Elements are not arbitrary. We have to find their reason."

"Is there a reason for your Reminda to have been killed?"

"You don't know if she is dead," Bobbien argued.

"Then where is she? How could they have let the boy king drown? He was beloved by all. The Elements don't exist. The only one you can depend on is yourself."

Bobbien turned on her. "So if that is true, then why don't you make Zayden see that depend on himself he must?"

"How? He is blind!"

"Only in his eyes," Bobbien told her cryptically. "A minor inconvenience." She left the hut and Denita to watch her shoulder her way through the crowd to the infirmary.

"A minor inconvenience," Denita repeated bitterly.

Chapter 3

Naje placed a hand on the wide swell of her belly, the child heavy in her womb. She looked out of the window of the palace, thinking how things had changed in so many ways in the past few months. The duals rays of the suns broke through the watery clouds. The Desa, so famed in the solar system for his vibrant red color, was a dull, matted brown. The lush forest looked like it had been clipped by a blade, the broken stumps giving it a desolate air. Naje looked across the vast horizon, searching for life. There used to be herns, gulls, and other waterfowl. The sky was still, the air turgid, a miasma of death hanging over the newly exposed hills and valleys. When she arrived here, it was a planet in transition. The small Plantan force took control with a vengeance. The planet's economy tanked with the loss of all the crystals during the invasion. The castle lurched; Naje grabbed the wall to steady herself. The great building groaned, the lights dimming for a minute, then righted itself. The city in the clouds was in trouble. The Randam Crystals that kept it flying high in the stratosphere, not doing the job. Supplies were stretched beyond their capacity. Her long nails tapped the wall, and Naje again wondered if she did the right thing returning to Darracia when Lothen went after them so many months ago.

Halfway to Venturian, Lothen's forces intercepted them with a peace offering. Sweet words, promises of grandeur seduced them back into the Plantan fold. Staf Neun, it seemed, was needed. Lothen stormed the castle after destroying the Desa, leaving the red forests of Darracia a smoking ruin. The Darracian council was imprisoned, and the leaders were replaced by Lothen's commanders. All of the Darracian nobility was ordered to the castle, but they too stayed away. Only with force, Lothen was able to bring them to his court, but they refused to bow to his rule. The Plantan population was limited; there were not enough of them to keep the planet running smoothly. They were actually the minority. It was as though they had captured a treasure ship but did not have the reserves to operate it. They needed the Darracian populace to cooperate. Lothen supplanted the Elements with the might of Geva, showing them a firestorm of her capabilities. He built impressive alters to her power but found few converts. Geva was a demanding goddess, her punishments cruel. There was nothing more than fear to motivate followers. He broke down the population one group at a time. The deportation of the rebellious Quyroos made the Darracians scared as well as submissive. Lothen used the vast resources of Quyroo slaves, exporting them to Bina to mine graphen for trade outside of their solar system. But he could not conquer by suppressing both species. The Plantan king realized the might of the Darracians would expand his empire. He needed to persuade them to join his army. The combined power of the Darracians, their Fireblade, and his Plantan warriors would soon control the entire solar system. There were thousands of trained warriors that would enhance by morphing his army into an unstoppable force. He needed them not as a conquered people but as the machine to mow down any opposition. The Quyroos were expendable, a perfect commodity to use to build a financial empire in the production of graphen. Once a species started using the drug, it was an unending source for income. No matter what he tried—coercion or brute force—Lothen couldn't break through the hard castle walls or Darracian hearts. Certainly Geva did her dirty work, but Lothen needed a populace that supported his visions of grandeur, not frightened into subjugation. A conquered species will ferment into rebellion. He had to turn them into a supportive population to build his far-reaching empire. Lothen needed a representative, one of their own to calm their fears, so they would join up to do his bidding. He had Seren, the Quyroo commander, keeping law and order on the planet surface. Malcontents were shipped out; only those who helped harvest Randam crystals were allowed to stay in the new holding camps they created. If they thought they were oppressed in the past, the future for any Quyroo looked bleak indeed. They were herded into huge camps where their every movements could be watched. All their freedoms were curtailed. Caught between being sent to certain death on Bina, many were relieved to be able to stay on Darracia, even if they were little more than slaves. The Darracians were necessary as his army. Strong, fearless, and stupid, they would make an unstoppable fighting force. The myth of that damnable Fireblade could be molded to turn his armed forces into a celestial fighting machine to conquer the whole solar system. He had to find someone to make the Darracians listen to him. He needed Staf Nuen. Lothen raced after their escape pod himself, leaving the planet in a hurricane of turmoil. He knew he had botched that part of his invasion. He expected to seduce his nephew V'sair into joining him. V'sair's bravery both surprised and irritated him. The young king's death was a waste. Losing Staf Nuen to his own ego was also not wise. He knew he better use more finesse in his politicking; otherwise his entire enterprise was in jeopardy. Naje could be the key to that success. He understood Naje, had used her well. Smiling, he remembered hot, sultry nights with her, before he gave her to Staf. He had seen her with her defenses down, her desires naked in her eyes. He shouldn't have given her away so quickly, she had uses still. He caught up with their escape pod and, with his oily charm, induced them to allow him to board in order to speak with them. Staf was more than useless, an addict. He could see the growing tension between the two lovers. The older man's shaggy head lolled against his seat. Naje paced the pod with a restlessness born from someone used to action. Lothen and Naje sized each other up in the small confines of the vessel.

"Come back with us," he said in a sibilant whisper.

Staf tried to unhook his seatbelt. "Not on your life, you stinking flounder!" he shouted, drool spilling from his slack lips.

Naje sneered at his face, disgust written all over her caramel features. It had not been an easy flight. Staf refused to shoot guns at the enemy. He was old, so he insisted on the honor of fighting with Fireblades. Naje turned away from both men, staring at the void of space before them. Its emptiness filled her with gloom. Instead of fighting the enemy, Staf fought her. She wanted to head for Chal Mala where a criminal overlord controlled that territory in the most outer planet of the solar system. If they offered support, perhaps the aging leader would make a new home base for them. Everyone traded information. She knew how to spin a story to make them both valuable. She had heard of this overlord. He was power hungry. She had planned to entice him into attacking Lothen. Instead, Staf insisted they go back to

Venturian. What was he thinking? She cursed. Didn't he know one must never go back? What did that icy rock have to offer? Did he expect to become a shopkeeper or meat stall owner? Maybe he wanted her to start over breaking her back in the graphen dens again. What future was there for her child, kicking furiously in her womb? She spun to look at the two males in the tight quarters. Staf's eyes rolled in his head, then narrowed to yellow slits. He loosed one arm, waving it at Lothen.

"You think you have me, my lord?" he growled. "I can fillet you like a slimy fish. You're scum, coming in and destroying the Desa. What were you thinking?"

Lothen smiled, his forked tongue flickering. "Oh, your grace?" He bowed respectfully. "I lost my head. See, I need your courage and brilliance to help me guide the people of your planet. My inexperience interfered."

"Naje!" Staf yelled, fumbling with his seat belts holding him captive. "Release me now, so I may talk to this puppy." He screamed her name when she failed to respond. Stalking over to him, she unlatched the buckle, watching him slide out of the deep chair to weave over to Lothen.

"You thought yourself too smart." He pointed a gloved finger to his head. "You need me, Lothen. You can't control the Darracians without one who unnderstan's them," he slurred.

"Staf!" She tried to make him stop. "He's…"

"You think to tell me what to do?" He rounded on her. "I am king! You know nothing of kingship. You are a woman, not even royal at that."

"Your Majesty." Lothen's words slithered in the small room. "Forgive me; I got caught up in the heat of battle. Surely you must sympathize," Lothen's voice was smooth,, but his eyes never left Naje. They followed her around the confined space saying, "See girl, look what you left me for."

Naje understood. She watched Staf strut around the room, directing her once again like a slave. "Get our things, Naje. We return home." He looked out the porthole.

"It's in the other direction, my lord," Naje told him sarcastically.

"No matter." He dismissed her. "We are allies once again?" He held out his arm to Lothen who took it in his tight grasp.

"We were never enemies, your highness. We had a miscommunication only."

"Naje, what say you?" Staf called out, his face alert once again. Naje wavered for a minute. Just how much was he aware, after all, she wondered. "Do we return to take our rightful place? You will be a queen," he stated baldly, challenging the other man in the room.

Lothen wondered who really held the power here: Naje with her hard heart and cool head or Staf with the heat of his Fireblade and its mythical powers. Naje nodded to Staf, who grunted. "So we return."

The one who held the power was Naje, the woman, he realized, observing her silently. Staf blustered, ordered, but ultimately let the woman decide. He may bully her, make her appear subservient, but Lothen watched their dynamics. Staf was an empty bag of wind, filled by Naje's quiet influence. Promises were made, and Lothen now understood the way to Staf was through Naje. She would be queen, he assured them both; however, Staf had to take one of Lothen's daughters as second wife, he argued. Lothen remembered Naje's hunger, her desire for her own power. He understood what she both needed and wanted to hear.

Later, they stood together in his own royal quarters, negotiating. Staf Nuen slept in a gray fog of graphen in another room.

"Why should we stay, my lord?" Naje stood tall, her caramel skin glowing in the early stages of her secret pregnancy.

Lothen walked over to Naje, taking her chin into his long bluish fingers. "You liked me once." His fingers caressed the soft skin of her arm. Lothen narrowed his smokey eyes, his lips touching the nape of her neck. He wrapped his muscled arms around her body.

Naje pulled away, her face disgusted. "You used me."

"We all use each other," he said as he poured himself a drink. "Nuen is an addict. Make it easy for me, and I will see you properly rewarded." He held out the drink, watching her intently.

"How do I know I can trust you?" Naje came closer to take the drink he offered. She put it to her plush lips but did not drink. "You threw me away. I have made the most of my new situation. I don't need you anymore."

"With him?" Lothen laughed. "Nuen is useless."

Naje watched him carefully. "I like him. He makes me feel like a woman." She thought for a minute, choosing her words carefully. "He needs me," she said with an indifferent shrug.

"You compare him to me?" Lothen lifted his arched brow. He pulled her against him, so she could feel his turgid flesh. He rested his hips against hers, brushing lightly, his lips grazing her lower cheek, his forked tongue flicking her earlobe. His breath tickled her, sending shivers of pleasure up her spine.

"You are breeding," he whispered intimately.

Naje spun away. "No!" She covered her belly protectively.

"Yes, I can tell. Your son will be king of Darracia." He walked up to pull her against him. He pressed himself intimately into her, letting her remember his arousal. Naje stood rigid but took a sip of his liquor, allowing it to warm her insides. She leaned her head backward, closing her eyes.

"You would let that happen? How can I trust you?" she asked quietly.

Lothen swallowed the bitter liquor in one gulp, laughing. "Oh, I think you can, Naje. In fact I know you can." He spun her around to face him, placing his mouth over hers possessively. Naje tore her face from his, but Lothen touched her cheek gently, his eyes burning bright with passion. "Naje," he whispered.

It didn't take much after that. They returned to Darracia, landing triumphantly, and with great fanfare. They stepped onto the smoking ramparts of the castle, Staf promising safety and peace. Was he not of the Darracian royal family? Staf invited the families back, doling out titles, knowing just what the noble class must hear. Using family ties, old friendships, he reassured them that life would slowly go back to normal. He promised them anything they wanted, just to return and support the new regime. Warily, the ruling families appeared at court. They admired Staf Nuen's Venturian woman. She charmed them with her beauty and devotion. Naje created a group of ladies that surrounded her, and together with Lothen's silent support, she selected couples of Plantan warriors and Darracian maidens. Soon, most of the major houses had foreign masters ruling theirs. Many of the Darracian sons were given high posts in the new army Staf formed under the guidance of the Plantan conquerors. Rebels found themselves quickly dispatched to transports to die in the graphen mines. Darracia was a changing planet.

Naje sat with Staf Nuen, doling out enough graphen to make him pliable to work with Lothen. She was respected now, necessary to diffuse the situation when Staf grew difficult. Naje understood how to spin the words into a shimmering net of compliance, so Staf went along with every plan. He sat on the king's throne, urging Darracians to embrace the Plantan invaders. Though these proud species were defeated, the actions allowed the illusion of freedom to fool them into obedience. The rape of Darracia had begun.

Quyroos retreated to the forbidden Eastern Provinces, where no one ventured safely. The ones that had stayed behind were exported to the mines on Bina to die on the high cliffs. The court became a dangerous place, where a loose tongue could cost a family its fortune as well as their home. Anyone who objected to the new rules disappeared the next day, along with their entire families. Staf sat on the throne, Naje next to him, and Lothen's pig-faced daughter to his left, the blue-skinned girl now in the early stages of pregnancy. Naje hated the girl, seeing her as a rival for Staf's attentions. He was easily persuaded, and if not for her careful regulation of graphen, who knew who would control his mind.

That was the key to her agreement. She was the sole distributor of graphen on Darracia, the new drug of choice. All vendors had to go through her to get orders. It made her rich beyond her wildest dreams. Kraynum, the distilled liquor was outlawed, and if one wanted a narcotic, they had to buy directly from Naje. She had security, money, status, and finally power. Naje narrowed her cocoa eyes to scan the hostile audience. They bowed to her now, the flowers of Darracian nobility. Of her sister, she thought not at all. She had enabled her to escape. More than that, she closed her heart. She had to worry about herself and her little one now. She laughed, looking at the smiling faces of the conquered. Lothen had cut them off at the head, these cloud people who thought themselves the most superior in the solar system. Who was superior now, she wanted to ask them? The Quyroo slaves left to service the ruling class were under the iron thumb of Seren, the native turncoat who basked in Lothen's good will. He ruled his nether kingdom on the murky red soil of the planet, keeping the Randam coming to power Syos, the cloud city. The Quyroo commander had the girl, Tulani. Naje had heard of her beauty but had never seen her. It was said she was imprisoned, until she willingly submitted to her captors. "Stupid girl," Naje thought bitterly, looking at the angry gray faces of the Darracians. Submission was easy. She laughed inwardly. Appearances were everything. Once one gave the illusion of subservience, gaining trust, nothing mattered. Naje smiled, her white teeth stark in her caramel face. She understood the secret and kept it close to her brittle heart. Protect yourself; do what one must. Success means nothing without survival. She caressed the infant, the heir, under her skin. She possessed the future of Darracia in her growing womb.

Chapter 4

Denita watched Zayden from the window of the hut. She placed the food on a heavy leaf, then picked her way through the muddy, red soil to where he sat under the janjan tree. The wide leaves protected them from the worst of the weather, but she shivered. She moved close to his bulk, hoping he'd warm her. Placing her cold hands underneath his tunic, she warmed them against his hot flesh. Closing her eyes, she leaned her face against him, remembering the safety she once felt him his arms.

"Go away," he told her tonelessly.

Denita ignored him. "I brought you food."

"Take it away. Give it away. I want to die."

Denita crawled in front of him so that she faced him. "Why? Do you think yourself half a man?"

Zayden laughed, "Half? I am nothing, not a shell. Save yourself, because there is nothing left here for you."

"I don't believe that," Denita told him, her lips close to his ear.

"I am dead."

"You told me that once before, Warrior, and we both learned that was untrue."

Zayden sighed, turning his face away. She could have been a tree or a rock, the way he shut her out.

Denita touched his face, running her hands through his disordered curls. The tattoo she made on his bicep gleamed wetly in the firelight. She traced it with her fingertip. "You are mine, Warrior. Nothing will change that."

Chapter 5

The trip to Bina had taken forever. Tied onto a metal bench with other prisoners, Reminda at first refused to eat. She wanted to die. She must have gotten close, because she remembered little of the journey. Feverous, she lay in her own waste, her face against the cold wall of the ship, her hands clenched in shackled fists. The Plantan guards forced food though her resisting mouth, beating her until she automatically opened her lips, her eyes swollen shut. It was cold. Her blue skin grew pale, and she wished for the Elements to take her to peace. She tried to call her husband's name; nothing but garbled nonsense filled her ears. Her gills grew infected, pus gathering in the folds, making breathing difficult. She wheezed, trying to become smaller, so she could slip away to the warmth of Drakko's arms. Her dreams were of darkness, of murky water, the pressure of the weight of it, squeezing what was left in her lungs to bubble out in a shallow exhale. Everything hurt—her arms, her legs, her head.

She became aware of a softness, a hand brushing back the tangles of her white hair, the gentle pressure of fingers parting her lips to dribble fluid onto her parched tongue. She rejected it, but he persisted, caressing her face to urge her with soothing words to drink.

"My queen, my queen." She heard the voice filling the corners of her brain, refusing to let her hide. "You must drink, please, my queen…" Sometimes it was playful, reverent, others insistent with a forced cheerfulness that made her want to strike the speaker with impatience. The murkiness parted, and she saw her head was in the lap of a giant Darracian, his gray face kind, his fingers tracing her face. He had a vicious slash down one side of his face. Reminda tired to rise, but he held her down, relief evident in his face. He had bright green eyes, so reminiscent of her husband that her breath caught, and he asked her, "Are you all right, your highness?"

Reminda rose slowly, her breath hissing in pain as her scabbed gills tore.

"Easy, my lady." He helped her up to rest against his huge chest comfortably.

It was presumptuous of him, yet Reminda found she didn't have the energy to mind.

"Do I know you?" she asked with as much dignity as she could muster in her weakened state.

"I'm not sure." He smiled, revealing rows of pointed Darracian teeth. "The guards have been kind enough to allow me to take care of you." He ducked his head. "They feared your were dying."

She realized he was older than she first thought. He had a Darracian royal braid, and she blinked in recognition.

"Colonel Brend?"

He nodded, adjusting her so she folded into the wall of his chest. His large hand reached over to pull her face inward, his fingers forcing her eyes to close. She heard his voice, suppressed in anger, muffled by the wall of muscle she was leaning on.

"What'd ye want now! She's still out, your great bastard."

Reminda went limp against him to give truth to his exclamation. She felt a baton prod her, steeling herself not to respond to the shock that followed contact with her tender skin. Instead, she felt her protector shove the baton away from her. It sizzled when it made contact with his skin. The air filled with the smell of scorched flesh.

"You've done enough. If you expect her to live to Bina, you better start listening to me."

Though his large hand covered her ears, she heard a smattering of the response. Words like *royal* and *Lothen* filtered through the barrier, and the sting of the electric shock did not come. Reminda let out a gusty exhale, as the echo of the guard's feet moved in another direction. She lifted her head to study her guardian once again.

"I do know you," she said quietly.

"I am honored."

"You are Swart's son."

Brend bowed his head. He saw her look at his royal braid, a question in her blue eyes.

"My mother was…" He touched his braid. "Princess Pavia."

"Drakko's great aunt."

"I was in your husband's honor guard." His eyes grew dark. "I now am yours."

"Your hand?" She looked at the burnt skin.

He waved it negligently. "It is nothing. I've had worse." He smiled gently.

Reminda had a vague memory of this man, always in her husband's great shadow. Drakko had hundreds of cousins. Most of the Draccian nobility was connected through marriage. Reminda hardly noticed anyone as Drakko eclipsed everyone in her eyes. The man was a few years her junior. Reminda lowered her eyes, suddenly uncomfortable in his arms. Sensing her shyness, Brend propped her against the bulkhead, turning to the next prisoner to say something. She felt the air change around them, heard the chains clanking against the metal with purpose as a murmur of excitement changed the texture of the air. Whispers filled the confined space mixed with fumbling until a small feast was lowered to the floor next to her. Reminda's blue eyes widened with question.

"We are all your honor guard now, your highness."

In the darkness, she made out the eager faces of Darracian soldiers, their hands clasped, with smiles lighting the gloomy darkness.

"We have prayed for your recovery." With clumsy hands, Brent unwrapped small portions of stale food that had been hidden in anticipation of her awakening.

"I can't take this…" Reminda shook her head. "You all need your sustenance to survive."

"We cannot survive without you, my lady." The soldier next to Reminda bowed his head. "Please eat the food."

Reminda heard the soft words of the guards whispering back to her like a hushed prayer. "Please…. please…" echoed off a hundred lips. She didn't need to see their satisfied smiles when she chose life and began to eat.

Chapter 6

Staf Nuen paced the Orbitous chamber, the conference table empty. Weak rays of light filtered through the gloom. He stopped to stare at the destroyed forests of the Desa, angry with both Lothen and Geva for the wasteful destruction. The ceaseless rains continued making the roads impassable. Work crews were inexplicably getting thinner and thinner. The door opened. His adjunct, a narrow-chested Plantan boy, entered, his Darracian armor swimming on his thin form. "We are arming children," Nuen thought with disgust.

"Your Majesty," the boy said, interrupting Staf's musings. "Your Majesty, Commander Seren to see you."

"Seren?"

"Commander of the Desa is his title, sir."

"What Desa? There's nothing left," Staf grumbled. "What does he want?"

The youngster cleared his throat. "I, ahem, I didn't ask."

Staf rounded on him, walking forcefully to backhand him mightily. The young man fell to his knees, cowering on the floor. "Next time ask. Send him!"

Seren was ushered in to stand tall before his Darracian liege. They eyed each other casually, two stalliuses measuring the opposition. Staf broke contact first to walk back to the window. He gazed at the darkening sky. "Commander Seren?"

"Your Majesty." Seren bowed deeply, so deeply it bordered mocking.

The air barely stirred. Staf rested his gloved hand against his thin lips, his yellowed eyes narrowed. "Who gave you, a lowly Quyroo, the Desa?"

"Your Majesty knows; it was Lothen."

"And why did Lothen give you the Desa?"

Seren had an idea of where this was going, but wavered on how to answer the king. He didn't like Neun. He had killed his uncle Jonis, who was head of the Quyroo league when he overthrew Drakko, the last king. He had a blood feud to settle with him. Yet, for all his sins, Nuen loved Darracia, and the planet was in trouble.

"For services rendered." At last he responded to Staf.

Staf turned to look at him, his face set like iron. "Services for whom?"

Seren shifted uncomfortably, he understood what Staf was going to say. There would be no help from his quarter. "Today, the Office of Justice slid onto the Hills of Terun." He moved closer to Staf. "Look, you." He pointed out into the cloudy gloom. "The Secondus Residential Building is hovering over the Hixom Sea."

"So…"

"So, your city in the clouds is falling. It's falling on my…I mean, on the Desa."

Staf shrugged indifferently; Seren went on. "Lothen is a mad man. He is transporting all my…the Quyroos. If I don't have a workforce, we cannot find the crystals."

"Take it up with Lothen."

"I have. He says I must make do with what I have."

The building shifted, gears moaning. Both men rolled on the balls of their feet as the building leveled. Staf used his tail to gain balance. Seren walked close to Staf. "You see. The crystals are failing. I can't find enough to replace them."

Staf reached into his pocket to take out a graphen blossom with a pipe. He stuffed the pipe and lit it, his eyes never leaving Seren. "You made your bargain with the devil. Now abide by it."

Seren threw up his hands in frustration. "Why did you come back here?"

"Not to help Quyroo scum like you," Staf told him.

"You are allowing them to destroy our home!"

Staf turned to stare out the window bleakly, wondering why indeed he came home.

Chapter 7

Food was shoved through the cell door to splash against the wall. Tulani eyed the mess with disgust.

"Eat it, you red keywalla," the guard said, sneering. He pushed his baton through the cell, catching Tulani under her chin to hold her face flush to the iron bars. The rusty residue ground into her cheek scraping her sensitive skin. Pinpricks of electricity needled her skin. Gritting her teeth, she refused to show pain, and the guard laughed, leaning close to her. Her red braids hung in a tangled mess down her back. Her clothing was in tatters. She had been in this filthy cell for weeks. Half starved, her bones accenting her thin cheeks, she closed her eyes forlornly.

"I can make it easier for you here, girl." He licked his blue lips with a reptilian tongue. "I can come to you tonight with food." He reached in to caress her chest. Tulani turned to memorize his face, knowing when she got out she would kill this person.

"I would rather lie with a jast," she said through gritted teeth. Despite the dryness in her mouth, she found enough moisture to spit in his face.

Her jailor jerked the cudgel to glance off her cheek, her jaw cracking from the blow. He wiped his face, his eyes never leaving hers. "I will make you pay tonight. Even a jast won't want you when I get finished with you."

He stormed off, leaving Tulani to slide down the cell wall to the floor.

Seren had put her there, when she refused to cooperate. She remembered that fateful day when she watched V'sair fall to his death in the Hixom Sea. Tulani stood on the ramparts of the great castle wall, screaming, her heart broken. They had hauled her in after they surrendered, sat in silent grief, mute with shock at the mindless violence when Reminda's brother Lothen took control of the planet. The Desa smoked, violated from the constant bombardment, the high tree homes of her species destroyed. The vast population of the Quyroos, both tree dwellers and bottom dwellers, either dead or scattered on the smoking planet. The gaping hole of Aqin—a raw, weeping wound, silently crying at the loss of Ozre. The volcano was leveled, its walls blown apart by Geva, the evil goddess worshipped by Lothen and the Plantan invaders. Tulani stared at the colorless sky, her home ruined, her people systematically enslaved, the Darracians powerless to fight the new ruling class of the planet.

Swart and Vekin along with any Darracian with a pretense of rebellion were deported to the graphen mines, to die on the high cliffs. Transports left daily. She watched them herd captured Quyroos onto the huge ships to be sent to certain death on Bina.

She was sent to the surface of the planet with a mixed group of captives to be deported on the next transport. They waited in the Plains of Dawid, which had been transformed into a crude marketplace. Rutted streets were flanked by makeshift stalls. Shopkeepers had come up with inventive ways to keep the ever-present rain off their product. Many had used the wide leaves from the janjan tree woven together as a covering, bringing a pang of homesickness to Tulani. Others used hammered metal, the constant rain adding to the deafening noise. Tulani's head ached from it. Her feet sunk into the loamy soil up to her ankles. Soon her dress was plastered to her body, her skirt heavy with water. The fine mist created a hazy blur of the planet's surface. Everything was wet, the wreckage of the rotted trees giving off an offensive smell of decay. It was crowded. Plantans, Darracians, and other species packed together in a teeming maze of streets. Most of the Plantans were armed, and the Darracians had the bleak eyed worried stares of the conquered. Now they knew what it felt like to be insecure in your own home. Confidence belonged to those who felt safe. Strangely, confidence too belonged to those who didn't care. She understood that feeling well. She scanned the crowds, looking for a familiar face. No one knew yet if her grandmother survived. There was nothing to live for anyway, and Tulani wished for death. Her eyes were hollow, especially after she watched the invaders kill V'sair's jast, roasting him whole in the fireplace in the throne room. They were barbarians, with no respect for life except their own. In fact, she observed them fighting among themselves, murdering with abandon in duels over loot. She had always known prejudice, had seen unfairness in the way the Darracians treated Quyroos, but this took suppression to a whole new level. She was in a line, waiting to be stamped, then loaded, when a hand pulled her out of the formation, throwing her onto the wet red ground.

"You there!" A Plantan official stomped over. "What do you think you're doing? She's scheduled for the next deportation to Bina."

"She's mine." A hated voice filled her ears. Tulani stood to get back into the line. Seren put his foot on her thigh, his hand imprisoning hers. "I have been searching for you and that disgusting hag, your grandmother."

"I belong to no one," she told Seren. "Bobbien lives?" she added, hope lighting both her heart and star-shaped eyes.

"You belong to me, Tulani." Seren gripped her wrist. "The king is dead, and your grandmother is missing. You've led me on quite a chase." He sneered, his red face dripped with moisture. He wiped at it with his other hand. "You'll be coming with me now, Darracian slattern."

Tulani resisted against his hand. "You're hurting me."

Seren laughed. "Get used to it."

He pulled her toward his stallius tethered to a post nearby. It was white, as pure as the color of V'sair hair. Tulani's eyes filled as she whispered, "Hother." Her heart broke.

"Yes, like Hother, you will be mine as well." Seren dragged her.

"Hey, Quyroo! You can't just take one of them like that!"

Seren spun, pulling Tulani as he approached the Plantan guard. "Do you know who I am? Do you? Do you? I am Seren, the district commander of the Desa."

Seren pulled out his sword, menacing the other man. The Fireblade was a dull orange, humming deeply. He raised his arm to attack, when a shout stopped him.

Lothen, King of the Planta, rode up on a black stallius. He was surrounded by his elite guards.

"Seren, my good friend, what goes on here? Ah, you desire this female?" Lothen had seen the Quyroo commander stalk over to the transport line. He was a hothead, but a necessary hothead. He helped fight the Quyroo rebels and organize the work gangs on the planet. With his network of informants, he brought into vital information, squashing rebellion before it took root. There was a strong cell of fighters that evaded them. Well-coordinated skirmishes destroyed two supply trains, taking out boxes of the vital Randam crystals. Stocks were running low, and already the great city in the cloud's lights were dimmed. Due to the destruction, the interruption of war, everything was limited.

It seemed the only thing this world had in abundance was the graphen that Naje imported. Though he made a small tax from Naje's horde, the power for everything was the crystal. He had been too hasty in his attack, destroying many trees. He needed Seren to organize the harvesting of the crystals. Without the crystal, the city would fall, along with his power.

Seren spun, his rage subsiding. "This is Tulani. This man was disrespectful." He pointed to the guard who challenged him.

"The girl you were searching for? Well, you must take her." He needed Seren quiet. He was rounding up Quyroos for him daily to ship out to replace the ones dying on Bina. He also ran the work groups searching for the crystals. Seren ruled the ground with ruthless coercion keeping the supply to the minimum he could survive with. His attack had destroyed most of the trees that produced the sap that kept the city floating in the clouds. He needed the experts to search out the surviving trees to find the valuable commodity. Seren saved the hardest workers from the transports by offering them and their families a home in hastily made internment camps as long as they hunted out the crystals. Many jumped at the chance to keep their clans together. Bina was certain death. Hope remained still on Darracia. Lothen turned to the guard. "We do not treat our treasured allies like this." Lothen reached for his gun, blasting the guard's head off.

He bowed his head to Seren. "I will never forget your role in the invasion. Take your prize and celebrate."

Seren saluted the king with his sword. Dragging her to his new home, he proudly showed her his domicile. He had commandeered the old council building, furnishing it with whatever his men could steal. He had turned a cellar into a prison, threatening Tulani she would rot there if she didn't cooperate.

At first, he locked her in a chamber, sending servants, former daughters of noble Darracians to bathe and dress her. The large clothing swallowed her lithe form. Tulani stared out of the barred window, allowing them to comb and braid her long red hair. The food they brought in lay untouched. Seren arrived at dusk, slapping his gloves in the darkened room. "Tulani!" he barked.

Tulani sat in the dark shadows, ignoring his call. He called her again, walking in to light the many tapers so the gloom dissipated.

Seren pulled her into his rough embrace. Tulani turned her face, her gaze distant. With rough fingers, he gripped her chin, bruising her tender flesh to press his mouth against hers. Tulani tasted blood. Her eyes stared at Seren with hatred. Seren backed his face away to examine her. Tulani wiped her lips disgustedly with her wrist.

"Am I not good enough for the High Priestess? I am an important man now." Seren paced the room. "Tulani, join me as my woman. I am hoarding the crystals. Lothen will have to grant me a higher office."

"You are allowing them to transport our people."

"Only the weak, the injured. I am keeping the strongest here. I am building an army, an empire."

"You disgust me." Tulani eyed him with distaste. "V'sair was good to you. You turned on him."

"Crumbs!" He grabbed Tulani by her thin shoulders. "He gave us crumbs. I am no man's servant. V'sair was ineffectual. He couldn't get the planet united. What did he do for us?" Seren tossed her into a chair, imprisoning her there. Tulani covered her ears, and he used his large hands to hold them in her lap, forcing her to hear. "He did nothing for us!"

"He was a good man!" Tulani shouted, her face red, her cheeks wet with tears.

"He was a boy! Now you will see what a man can achieve."

"You are not a man but a coward," Tulani told him quietly, her face impassive.

He grabbed her pressing his lips against her. "You will feel a man, Great Sradda willing."

Tulani ignored him. Seren shook her, her braids falling around her body like a cape. Seren grabbed a hank of her hair, violently grinding his lips against hers. This time Tulani bit his lip, drawing blood. Seren backhanded her so that she fell against the hard-packed walls of the earthen room. He stalked over to her, lifting her by her hair and slapped her again.

"Like your men blue better?"

"You're not a man," Tulani said through gritted teeth. Her nose bled freely, her eyes bright in her face. "You are a beast. I don't couple with animals."

Seren roared, coming at her with both hands raised, when his father Jokin burst into the room.

"Stop, you fool!" He banded his arms around his son's chest. "She is worthless to us dead."

Seren screamed with rage, but his father held fast. "Think, son; you now have power. What would a leader do?" He shook him. "What would a leader do? Nuen rejected you. You need Lothen. We need Lothen. Think! Use her to your advantage; you could smoke out her grandmother and make a present of her to Lothen. Forget about Staf Neun. Lothen for all his sins has been better to you."

"Bobbien?" Seren asked, his breathing ragged.

"She's been succoring the Quyroo. She has created a camp where they are mobilizing, trying to build a force to eventually attack us. Think what it would do for you in the Plantans' eyes if you present Bobbien's head on a platter. You would have single handedly stop the rebellions."

Seren calmed enough, so his father let him go. "Send her to the cellar. Keep her there and let the word get out. They will mount an attack to rescue her, and then we strike."

"No!" Tulani raced to the door, but Jokin took his staff, hitting her on the back of her skull, knocking her senseless. Tulani slid to the floor, her eyes rolling back in her head.

"Yes, we will stamp out the rebels and make a gift of them to Lothen. You might rise to Grand Mestor."

"Lothen is Grand Mestor. He has brought back Staf Nuen as king."

"Staf Nuen is dying. They are killing him with graphen. Lothen will be king by the next moon phase, as soon as he assimilates his kinsmen into the Darracian culture."

"There is no room for the Quyroos."

Jokin kicked Tulani's silent form with his foot. "It is time for you to mate. Mate with a Plantan and dilute your Quyroo blood. In a few generations, there will be no Quyroos left but for the museum. Don't waste your seed on one such as this. She will get you nowhere."

Seren grunted in agreement. Tulani was not appealing lying on the floor, her face bloodied. His father had a point. Tulani was important when V'sair sat on the throne, but V'sair was dead and buried in the Hixom

Sea. It was time for him to find a new way to climb a ladder to the city in the clouds.

"Take her downstairs," he told a passing guard. "Lock her up. Keep her there until I tell you otherwise."

The withered old Darracian lifted the girl by her arms to drag her downstairs."

"Bait," his father said as he nodded.

"Yes, bait. Let's see what she attracts."

Chapter 8

V'sair came awake with a violent start, rising off a soft pallet. He took a deep breath, his nostrils flaring, as he gasped, realizing he was not underwater but in a warm, dry chamber. It was made from red granite, not unlike his home in the clouds. He looked curiously around, noticing there were no windows. The surface of the wall was rough and unfinished, carved from solid rock. It had a high ceiling, and strange violet shadows danced along its surface, undulating like the waves of the ocean. It was quiet, V'sair touched his ears, wondering if they were affected. They felt clogged, as if fluid was stuck inside. Shakily, he rose, the room spinning, his fingers lightly gripping the soft quilt. He picked it up, and holding it, he recognized it was made from the skin of a great fish. It had been treated, softened, but it was fashioned into a blanket. He wobbled over to a small table that had a plate of food. Small bits of fish were cut up and served with stewed red seaweed. V'sair's mouth watered, and he grabbed the food, shoving it into his mouth, enjoying the savory flavor as the food hit his empty belly.

A tall glass of liquid was next to the plate. It was faintly alcoholic, like a fermented beverage—sour, but satisfying. He gulped it down, his thirst quenched. V'sair strength slowly returned to his young body, his reserves replenished. The door opened, revealing a tall, blue-skinned man with masses of white hair. They looked so much alike that V'sair blinked and put the cup back on the table, leaving a small amount in the bottom.

"You must finish that, young sir!" the man said in a friendly way, gesturing the drink. "You need the fluids." He was dressed in pants made from the same iridescent skin as the blanket, but his blue chest was bare. He was older, perhaps Drakko's age. The hair receded on his forehead at each of his temples, and V'sair's hand automatically went to his own head.

"It's uncanny, it is." The man smiled, revealing pointy white teeth. "Let me see. We share white hair, blue skin, and a forked tongue."

V'sair shook his head and displayed his Darracian tongue. "Who are you?"

The older man smiled kindly. "Ah, but you do have gills, too." He gestured to V'air's chest with a webbed hand.

V'sair raised his shirt to watch his newly formed gills struggle with weakness.

"They are underdeveloped, but that will change the longer you stay here." The older man nodded.

"I cannot stay here," V'sair stated firmly.

The man shook his head, but his face remained friendly. "You will get used to them," he responded heartily.

"I cannot stay here. I have to go back to my home, sir. Please, where am I?"

"Oh no, no, young man." He smiled sadly. "I am Ovie, by the way." He took V'sair's wrist between his thumb and forefinger, encircling it. "Now do that to me. That is our greeting. You cannot leave here. You have seen us. You will give us away." V'sair lightly circled the older man's wrist, politely returning the greeting.

"You have my word that I won't reveal your presence, but I have to go home," V'sair informed him, his voice more forceful.

"No! Your home is here now. You will not leave here. Once you have seen us, it is, I fear, impossible. You will get used to us. There is great unrest on the surface anyway, now. It is not safe for either of us," Ovie replied with agitation.

"You don't understand." V'sair came to face him. "I am the king of Darracia. I have to go and save my people."

"You are king of nothing. The Plantans have destroyed your home. You have no home."

"You are Plantan," V'sair shot back.

"Oh no, no, no. We are descendants of the same species that peopled Planta eons ago. We call ourselves Welks. We are very different from them. While the Plantans developed outside the ocean, we have stayed underneath. We don't choose to mix with the species above ground. You'll see. You'll be happy here. We live in a peaceful society here. The Elements have made it so, Here Ereth answers our prayers."

"Ereth?" V'sair asked.

"Yes, come. I will show you."

They left the chamber, walking through a passageway made out of the same rough-hewn rock. V'sair's eyes adjusted to the gloomy interior. He paused to examine the wall, noticing its craggy wall was dotted with fossilized crustaceans. His long blue fingers glided over the pitted surface.

"We are underwater?"

"Yes," the older man acknowledged.

"Where?"

"We are deep under the Hixom Sea. We have been here longer than you."

"You never go above."

"It is against the law. We have avoided your species for eons."

"Why?"

Ovie considered the best way to answer the stranger. "Because we don't trust you."

Mildly insulted, V'sair could find nothing to say in response to that. Ovie must have felt his embarrassment and shrugged. "It's nothing personal, you understand. It's just that you are…your species is so destructive. Come, the hour grows late. We are having an assembly to introduce you later today."

Without another word, V'sair considered what Ovie said, silently following him. Perhaps his species was too destructive.

They entered a huge cave, deep purple shadows painting the vast room. V'sair found it hard to believe he was underwater; it seemed the chamber went up endlessly. A giant waterfall taking up the entire right side of the cavern filled the room with a deafening roar. Water droplets misted the area, and soon V'sair's pale hair hung in a damp rattail against his wet back.

"Where is this place?" he shouted, but his voice was lost in the ceaseless pounding of the water. Licking his lips, he realized it was seawater. The entire right side of the room was a crystal wall, revealing the ocean floor. Cut into the rock, it served as a vast window to the ocean. V'sair's jaw dropped when Ovie waved his hand and lights backlit the area, revealing a multitude of fish—some the size of buildings, swimming lazily behind the polished quartz. V'sair walked over, placing his hand on the wall, his face in awe. Silently he stood, gazing at the bottom of the sea, the creatures on the other side ignorant of their observer.

"Humbling, isn't it?" Ovie commented with a wry smile. "Takes my breath away every time. Ah…" He smiled, his face lighting with pleasure as the female who rescued V'sair swam over to touch the glass over Ovie's hand on the other side. "My daughter, Hennith."

V'sair watched her float nearby, her webbed hand placed directly over his on the other side of the glass. "She is the girl who saved me." She swam backward, with a smile on her lips. A pink turtle floated by, and the girl mounted it like a stallius to ride in lazy circles.

"Yes, she was out on patrol. Usually we allow nature to take its natural path."

"I don't understand."

"We rarely rescue your kind or the red ones."

"The Quyroo," V'sair supplied.

"They're never happy here and want to return to land. We can't allow that."

"I don't understand why." V'sair turned to face him.

"You are destroyers. You don't give back to the planet. Take, take, take—always making changes. Why wasn't the land good enough for you? Instead you had to build cities in the sky. Taking crystals, making everyone work for them, always improving…"

"Improving is a good thing," V'sair said indignantly.

"To what purpose? Can one simply exist? Look." Ovie drew closer. "See my daughter. She swims everyday. She protects the ocean floor and our creatures. We take only what we need to survive. We replenish what we take. We live alongside all the creatures in this great sea, not oppressing or trying to change them."

"Darracians don't do that!"

"Oh I beg to differ, young sir." He held up his webbed hand. "One, you suppress the Quyroos. Two, you take the crystals to fly your home making a separation between species. Three, you create differences by claiming only some have the power to operate the Fireblade."

"That is not my belief. I learned the Fireblade is lit by the soul of its owner, and anyone can operate it."

"To what end? What is the importance of the weapon?"

"You have blades!" V'sair accused. "I saw the spears."

"Yes, because we have to protect ourselves from the likes of you!" Ovie spat.

The waterfall froze midair, and the room vibrated with intensity. Colors flashed around V'sair as a great rumbling rocked the floor.

"Enough!" a booming voice declared. "You see! You see what is happening? He is here less than a day, and you are bickering, fighting like the landwalkers."

Ovie fell to his knees before the back wall. The rocks squirmed, undulating as a roar shook the room. Small boulders bounced off the cliff, falling like gravel to land around the two men. V'sair dodged the rocks nimbly. His eyes scanned the giant wall; he stood stock-still realizing it went upward for several stories and was quite alive. He walked over to touch the red wall, communing with the being living in it. His eyes scanned up in disbelief. "Ereth?"

Chapter 9

The rain turned the Desa floor into a red quagmire impenetrable for the Plantans to pursue the escaping Quyroos. The hidden camp swelled as more Quyroos arrived daily. Sanitation became a problem. Bobbien could barely keep up with the influx of refugees. Tales of mass transportation of the species were told in the hushed, makeshift city of earthen huts. The rest that stayed were in internment camps, forced to hunt for crystals demanded by the conquerors. Thousands of crude homes were created, side by side, small cooking fires outside adding to the murky, wet haze. The air quality was poor, laden with moisture, combining with the smoke, to turn the pure atmosphere into a smoggy mess. Mold coated every surface; food rotted on the vines. Her people were starving, and she could find no answers in the prayers she voiced each night.

"Ozre, Ozre, why have you forsaken us?" She held great hanks of her long braids in her hand as she cried on her knees. She worried about the growing multitude of her people. She worried about Tulani. She worried so hard that she felt her heart beating with fear every minute of the day. They were disorganized. The joke was to put two Quyroo in a council and nothing would get accomplished. All they did was argue.

Her back ached from the long hours she worked, treating the outbreak of hufen just this week. Poor sanitation, coupled with lack of fresh water, made for a bad recipe of communicable disease. She hoped that Tulani was still in the castle, warm and dry. She traveled weekly to the marketplace in the Plains of Dawid for information about Tulani, but thus far, there had been nothing. Not a word about her granddaughter alive—or dead. The rain poured daily, making travel next to impossible. If only the incessant rain would cease. If only the growing population of displaced Quyroo could organize themselves into a fighting machine. If only Denita would stop babying that great hulk of a warrior so he could lead her people to victory. "If only," she thought, looking out the door where the girl sat next to the broken soldier that held the dreams of the future in his useless hands.

Denita sat beside Zayden silently, while he slept. She watched the rise and fall of his filthy tunic, his eyes closed, his face devoid of the new lines she noticed fanning from his amber eye.

He had been so silent today, she feared he was dead. A plate sat between them, his forgotten meal destroyed by the hungry bugs eating it. She had protected it for the longest time, giving up when he failed to answer her questions. How long could he mourn, she wondered. Blind, almost always drunk, she knew his life was over. His humor, and kind gallantry had fled when he lost his sight.

"I told you to go away." His raspy voice broke the stillness of the evening.

Denita ignored him, moving her behind settling in.

"I said I don't want you here!"

Denita held still, breathing lightly, thinking she would fool him into believing he was alone once again.

"Denita!" he shouted angrily. "I know you are here. I can hear you breathing." He turned to face her, his blind eye blazing with heat.

"You don't know that." She got up, stealthily moving before him staring at his sightless face sadly. She was inches from him but held herself as still as she could.

Zayden reached out, grabbing her wrist, twisting it in a merciless grip.

"You see me?" Denita gasped through clenched teeth. "Stop it, Zayden; you are hurting me."

"I told you to leave me alone…" He stood, dragging her upward. Slightly dizzy, he leaned heavily against a broken tree.

"You there!" Cosfar stomped toward them. "You are hurting the female."

He came in on Zayden's left. The big Darracian cocked his head, listening intently. Raising his leg, he expertly kicked the Quyroo in the stomach, sending his sprawling backward into a well of mud. It splashed them both, coating them with the red substance.

"You can see?" Denita asked wondrously, the pain of his grasp forgotten, her free hand traveling to touch his scarred cheek.

Zayden expertly knocked the hand away, before it even touched him.

"Don't be a fool. Your sister blinded me." He held her by the shoulders, shaking the helpless girl.

"She was protecting you."

"She destroyed me!" he roared. "I am useless to everybody now!"

Denita escaped his merciless hold, cupping his face with both her hands. "You are not useless to me, Warrior." She kissed him softly.

Zayden's cheeks were wet, and she brushed away the tears tracking down his face. He staggered away from her, tripping over a protruding root. Falling face first into the dirt, his arms sank into the mud to his elbows. Cosfar hooted with laughter.

"Denita, leave this beast and come with me. I will show you how a real man takes care of his female." Cosfar rose, grabbing Denita's arm in a vice-like grip.

"Leave me alone." Denita struggled with the big Quyroo.

"How long has it been for you?" Cosfar encased her in his arms, putting his mouth over hers. He ground his lips against her mouth, cutting off her curses.

Zayden's head turned to Denita's direction. "Denita?" he growled. The muffled cries were his only answer.

"You can't see me!" Cosfar yelled. "Slink off into the forest and stop being a drain on us."

Zayden cocked his head, listening for Denita. He tuned his head slowly, clicking his tongue against the roof of his mouth. His head did a slow scan, stopping directly in the line of sight of the couple. Zayden's amber eye glowed with heat. With a roar, he launched himself at the them, colliding with Cosfar with a resounding smash. His balled fist found Cosfar's face, his pebbled knuckles making painful contact with his nemesis's nose. Though the entire attack, Denita heard a steady clicking, wondering where it was coming from.

They scrabbled in the dirt, the thick mud coating their skin, blood dripping from both their faces. Cosfar gave as good as he got, making no concessions for Zayden's handicap. "Truth be told," he wondered, "what handicap?"

Bobbien saw the fray, launching herself between the two combatants, her strong arms pulling them apart. "Stop that, you big lukes! Supposed to fight the Plantans, we are. Not each other." She pushed Cosfar out of the way. Zayden clicked, spinning to follow him. A smile split her face, her star-shaped eyes watching the blind warrior follow his target. "Figured it out, have you?"

Zayden paused, turning in Bobbien's direction. "What are you talking about?"

Cosfar cautiously approached the two of them.

"Think you I put you under that dripping janjan tree for no reason?" Bobbien demanded.

Denita came up placing her arms around Zayden's heaving chest. "What did the tree do?"

"Nothing," Zayden answered. "The tree did nothing."

Bobbien laughed. "But the rain did its job, right, Zayden? The Elements have provided you a means to see." She nodded sagely.

"The rain?" Cosfar demanded.

Bobbien watched a grin grace the Darracian's face. "If you don't tell them, I will," she stated.

"Could it be true? Was it Ereth? Ereth is your Element of water?" Denita asked.

"Water is the birthplace of life. It makes the Desa grow."

"Too much rain can destroy," Denita told her.

"The Elements would never destroy! Ereth gives life. Sometimes you don't need anything but faith," Bobbien said softly.

"It wasn't faith, Bobbien. The rain fell in an auditory pattern around me. If I listen just right, I can hear it dripping. When I click my tongue against the roof of my mouth, the sound reflects back its location. That's science, old woman."

"If you say so, Zayden. Some may call it science. I choose not to."

"That was the strange sound I heard, those clicks," Denita interrupted.

"Like a whale or a bird, reflecting sound back is part of nature," Zayden spoke.

"Or a miracle," Bobbien added.

"He is still blind," Cosfar fumed. "He is of no use to us!"

"Says who? Have you forgotten the Elements?" Bobbien demanded. "Are your ears so full of anger and rain that you have lost your ability to believe? The minute you are challenged, you fold like wet laundry!"

"The Elements have deserted us!" Cosfar's face shook with rage.

A crowd developed, grumbling, calling for more to join them with Cosfar, Zayden, Bobbien, and Denita in the center. The rain dripped steadily, covering them all with moisture.

"Have they?" Bobbien returned, menacingly. "Or have they put obstacles in our path to test the depths of our faith? Are you so sure they have left?" Bobbien held up her hands in the gloom, "Let us rejoice! Spoken through this man, Ereth has. A miracle has happened. Close to death as it comes, he was, and Ereth has breathed life into him. Lead us to victory, he will." She grabbed Zayden's lax hand high, reaching with all her might to the tallest tree. "Unite, we shall! We shall unite to save our home!"

"Wait a second there, Bobbien. I'm blind. I can't…" Zayden whispered.

Cosfar took that opportunity to pick up a stick, swinging it toward Zayden. Zayden pulled away from Bobbien, spinning, his tongue clicking furiously—one hand catching the weapon, the other bunched fist clipping Cosfar neatly on the jaw.

Zayden stood over the unconscious Quyroo as he finished his sentence with wonder: "See."

Chapter 10

Naje lay on the divan, her hands rubbing the protruding mound of her belly with oil. She wanted her figure to return as soon as possible after the birth. The door opened, and Staf Nuen entered, his glassy eyes yellow with graphen, his pitted face grim. He sat down heavily next to her on the couch, waving out her attendants. They were in the Ambros room, Reminda's former court. Naje had changed the room from the airy and light reception room into a dark, shadowy place. Heavy furniture filled the space, the light from the wall of windows covered by thick dark drapes that trapped the air inside. She had always lived in a freezing home and vowed never to be cold again. The room was hot, fires built up beyond what Reminda used to have. Staf wiped the sheen of sweat that dotted his forehead. His tail drooped forlornly.

"Leave us!" he called out to her attendants.

Naje rolled over, as if to sit up, but Staf stayed her with a hand to her shoulder.

"No, I have missed you." He leaned forward to wrap her in his arms. She slid out of his embrace easily.

"Shouldn't you be in Temple with Lothen?" She pulled a graphen packet from her pocket. Flicking it with her forefinger, she walked to the table to pick up the ever-present pipe she kept in the room. She filled it expertly, bringing it to him, presenting it with both hands.

"I didn't come here for graphen. I came here for you." He rose to press against her, nuzzling her neck. Naje winced at his clumsiness. Wrapping her in his arms, he embraced her stomach from behind. "How is my son?"

Naje turned to face him. "He would feel both safer and better if his father was with Lothen. Think Staf. You allow Lothen to conspire with Geva!"

"Geva is a weak goddess." Staf dropped his arms, walking over to pour himself a glass of illegal Kraynum. He swallowed it, his throat burning from the heat of the liquor. Closing his eyes, he was transported in time to another meeting in the castle, when he plotted with his deceased wife Beatha to take the throne from his brother.

But he had the throne now. Staf Neun was king. King of what, though? Lothen had destroyed Darracia. Transports had denuded the population of Quyroos. Darracians now filled the roles as servants. Plantans held any position of power. He lured the nobility in, only to watch helplessly as Lothen raped the land, stealing titles for his people and marrying the Darracian females to his own limited supply of Plantans. Staf Nuen was king to a hostile population that was not even his own species.

"A weak goddess?" Naje rounded on him. "Stop speaking nonsense. She crushed your Elements."

"Element." Staf saluted her beautiful face. "Only Ozre was affected."

"What are you saying? Ozre is gone."

"He has disappeared for now, but there are three Elements. Didn't you read the book I gave you?"

Naje made a face. "I do not like to read."

Staf stalked to her side. "You have the future king of Darracia in your body, and you don't even understand our culture!"

"What culture?" Naje shouted. "You are a conquered people. Soon the Quyroos will be extinct. The Darracians are the new subspecies, the servants. Why would anyone want to worship their gods—gods that deserted them and allowed them to be vanquished? Not me, Staf, not me!" She turned to leave him alone, another graphen packet on the table for him to use.

"They're not gone," Staf said as he picked up the graphen to spill the dried blossom into his pipe. He lit it thoughtfully, sucking deeply, letting the drug envelope him. "Just sleeping, but none of you listen to me."

Chapter 11

By the time the slave transport reached Bina, a communication system had been developed between the prisoners. Colonel Brend was the highest-ranking officer on the ship. His careful nursing has helped Reminda get better. She was still weak. The food rations were meager, but somehow she had enough for her body to regain its strength. The Queen was quiet, watchful, her hooded eyes scanning the room. She said little, accepted no considerations for her status, and a quiet rapport between herself and the colonel had developed. As they neared Bina, she hid her anxiety. He had become a solid wall from the ugliness of life, and Reminda was used to his calm resolution, making her feel protected and cherished. His deep commitment and quiet strength reminded her of Drakko. She found comfort when her weary eyes rested upon his large form. The guards were lax. When one of his men succumbed to fever, they switched his clothing. Wrapping him in blankets, they called the jailors.

"The queen is dead. She has died from the fever."

"Uncover her."

"If I do," Brend told him, after a long bout of coughing, "it will contaminate the entire room. You will get the contagion."

The Plantan backed away. "Jettison her out of the rear hatch with the trash. Yes, yes, get rid of her quickly."

He had disguised Reminda, using bits and pieces from everyone's clothes. Her long white locks were cut close to her head with a contraband razor. Dirt rubbed into his skin to hide the color. She disappeared into the role created for her—a young teen, a servant, one of the great unseen who travel in the shadows. She was his squire, his younger cousin, he told the watchmen.

"Keep you face down," he told her, adjusting her shirt. He pulled a cap over her face, hiding the telltale tattoos. "I mean it. No matter what you hear, keep you face to the ground."

He placed her between two of the biggest Darracians as they exited the ship, getting her past the lazy guards and into one of the metal quarters set up for slaves.

"In a perfect world, my lady, you would be in an all-female room." He made her a bed in the bunk above his, tucking her between the blankets when the lights were extinguished.

"You have a plan?" she whispered in the dark. "Colonel…"

"Shhhh." He rose, to face her in the dark. He loomed above her in the dark, like a great bat, his wide shoulders blocking out whatever weak moonlight reached the room. "I think for safety you must call me by my birth name."

"That is highly irregular, Colonel."

"These are irregular circumstances. Marek. Call me Marek."

"That is for your family, your wife…" she whispered back.

He shook his head. "I have no wife. I will call you Minda."

Reminda watched his lips as he spoke, the words clogged in her throat. It was not that she was a prude; she prided herself on being rather progressive. It just wasn't done, and on top of it, she was the queen. Instead she found her lips breathlessly saying his name, Marek, as though she couldn't help herself.

He nodded in assent. "It is for safety only, my la... Minda. We have a plan." He reached out to touch her hand. Her knuckles were white, gripping the filthy blankets tightly.

The lights in the room burst on, and several Plantan guards spilled in. They had batons that they slammed the bunks with making a deafening racket. Reminda winced as they neared but slid down at the demands for them all to stand by their beds.

Marek stood slightly before her, his large bulk hiding her slight form.

"Stand too, you Darracian slime!" A tall, blue-skinned man screamed. He was accompanied by a Venturian male, elevated from slave to housemaster. "This is Unis." The Plantan pointed to the Venturian. "He is not your friend. You will obey him. He can make your life here easy or hard." He walked up and down the room, looking at each of the men. He stopped before Marek to stare at Reminda's downturned face. "What wrong with him?" He placed his baton under Reminda's chin. Sparks flew making Reminda's eyes water from the pain.

Marek placed a hand on the stick. "He is my squire, my cousin, a half breed."

"He looks…"

"Blue," Marek finished. "My aunt mated with a Plantan. I promised to keep him safe."

Their eyes locked as if they were taking each others measure. Marek shrugged. "He is simple. A blow to his head as a child. I promised."

"He will not last if he cannot keep up," the guard told him simply. He leaned forward. "Save his food for yourself and dump him at the cliffs. You'll do better without excess weight."

Marek's gray eyes locked with the blue ones. "I made a promise."

"Oh you and your Darracian code of honor. Let's see how strong you are to withstand the graphen mines. Let's see how long your ethics last there." He laughed as he walked out of the room. He stopped at the doorway to look back at Reminda once again, as she stood behind the great bulk of her protector. He smirked, tapped the wall with the baton, hitting the lights to throw them into darkness once more.

Chapter 12

Tulani rested her head against the bars of the cell, the light from the four moon bathing her face. The cell was carved in the red rock of the planet and jutted out over the Hixom Sea. She watched the churning waves below her, the white froth swirling in anger, the water choppy. A light breeze blew in from the sea, and she licked her dry lips tasting salt. She touched her face, realizing the salt was from the tears bathing her face. All was lost. V'sair, Reminda, Zayden were all dead. Life was over; she had no reason to live. She stared at the sky, the dim lights of Syos blurring in her eyes. She brushed at them, ashamed of her feelings, yet she was so alone. It was so quiet, the broken skyline of Aqin silent and dead, now that Geva had crushed the volcano. The raucous sounds of Quyroo encampments were still as a grave. Everyone was gone, silenced by the invasion, defeated by the parasites taking control of the once beautiful planet. All the problems, the issues Darracians and Quyroos fought over paled in light of the conquerors. The differences that divided the planet seemed insignificant. If only they had worked together, united, and stopped fighting over petty nonsense. She looked sadly at the smoking Desa, with its uprooted trees, broken like weak twigs, thousand-year-old trunks snapped like saplings. It was all gone, and she would have the rest of her life to think how she could have played it differently, using her resources to bond V'sair and herself, rather than polarize them.

The old man shuffled by her cell. "You do not eat the food."

Tulani shrugged, her eyes glued to the horizon out the window.

"You are Bobbien's girl?"

Tulani sniffed loudly, then nodded.

"I always liked Bobbien," he offered as he picked up her plate to take it away. "She was nice for a Quyroo. My name is Kovo."

Tulani stiffened, then turned to see if he was baiting her. He had kind eyes. He was a very old Darracian, way too old for this kind of work. "What do you mean by that?"

"If we understood what it meant to be a Quyroo, things might have been different is all." He heard his name called, and she noticed his gray skin paled. "You'll only hurt yourself if you don't eat. I will leave this after all." He placed the food next to her on the ground. "Eat it, child. Eat it for Bobbien."

Kovo backed out of the cell without another word.

Tulani considered his words and took a piece of fruit to nibble, while she stared absently at the silver surface of the sea. A ball of light spun across the top of the water. Tulani perked up, watching it zip in circles to come and rest on the waves. "Ozre?" she whispered. It grew larger, spreading out like a net of stars, blanketing the water. Tiny sparkling lights twinkled, reflected on her face. She pulled herself against the bars, hope blooming in her chest. She reached her hand through her cage as far as it could go. The small ball bounced on the waves, sending geysers into the tiny room. The seawater splashed Tulani, the fluid baptizing her, bringing the ghost of a smile to her face. "Sweet Sradda," she prayed, her chest filling with excitement. "Water means life. The Trivium is whole. One without the other is not whole. Creator to Ozre to Ereth to Ine-one is powerless without the other. Without them we are nothing." She finished the prayer. The lights winked in agreement, then slowly sank. She watched the illuminated water slowly grow dark as the constellation of lights descended toward the ocean floor. Cocking her head, Tulani digested what she just witnessed. The lights were blue. The orbs were Ereth.

Chapter 13

V'sair sank to his knees before the living rock, "I bow before the mighty Ereth."

The ground rumbled, but oddly, V'sair felt as safe as when he was in the volcano with Tulani and Ozre. He began the Songs of Sradda, the ancient prayer filling the giant space. His voice soared to the ceiling, his passion making him blind to all around him. At last, V'sair felt at peace. He was found, familiar, with something he understood. He sang the words his tutor Emmicus pounded into his head, finding solace in their message. He ended his prayer with a sigh, relief filling him, waiting for direction to come to him. A net of blue light shimmered above the chamber outside the glass wall. The balls of energy danced in the water in a synchronized ballet, a thing of beauty. Slowly, gracefully they descended into the giant vault, creating a spangled cloud around them. V'sair stood in wonder, noticing the both Ovie and his daughter Hennith were with him, their faces reflecting startled joy.

V'sair raised his arms, waiting to commune with Ereth, allowing him to invade his body. He was drenched; a fine mist surrounded each ball of rotating light. When the voice came, it vibrated inside the entire room.

"I am Ereth, Element of Life, born of the water."

"Ereth, Ereth, I commend myself to thee," V'sair responded.

"Well, you should." Ereth laughed. "Took you long enough to notice me."

"Notice you? What do you mean?" V'sair questioned.

"The rains? I tried everything—floods, mists, clouds, torrential downpours—yet none of you reached out. Silly, silly creatures."

"We were preoccupied," V'sair explained.

"To quote my good friend Ozre, excuses…"

"Ozre, is he well? Oh please say he is well. I saw Geva destroy him."

"Looks can be deceiving," Ereth told him cryptically.

"So," V'sair said simply.

"So," Ereth responded.

"I have found you."

"Yes, you have. What are you going to do now?"

"The Elements are the Trivium. The Elements are whole. Without them we are nothing," V'sair quoted the prayer. He turned to look at the others. "This is a sign. We have to go back."

"No!" Ovie yelled, moving close to the giant mountain. "I see only one Element: ours, the Element of water. The Trivium is not whole!" The room started to hum, the vibration coming from the hard rock under the soles of their bare feet. A spinning orb rocketed around the room, its color changed from white to red. Ovie ducked as it made to hit him.

"One does not have to see something to know of its existence!" The deep voice reverberated through the chamber.

"Ozre!" V'sair dropped to his knees, his arms spread in supplication. He could barely contain his joy, his relief. "Ozre, does my mother live?" he asked.

"Yes, but we must act quickly."

The two Elements hung suspended, the brilliance lighting the chamber. The stone wall was nothing but rocks, now, the Elements' power in the spinning orb.

"I don't understand." Ovie approached the ball. "We have heard of Ozre but were not sure of its existence."

"There are three Elements. Ozre, Ereth, and Ine. The Trivium is whole; one without the other is not whole." V'sair made the holy arc from his chest with his hands as he quoted the stanza of the song.

"One cannot exist without the other." The Elements responded to the prayer.

"Ozre, Ozre, light the path." V'sair paused thoughtfully. "Ozre, I thought Geva had destroyed you," V'sair said, his voice ending on a broken whisper.

"Pah, parlor tricks. She is a sham and will disappear when we have united land, sea, and air."

Hennith walked up, placing her finger into the center of Ozre's red depths. "Oh, Father," she said in shock. "He means to have us join the landwalkers."

"No, no, no." Ovie shook his head. "We do not go there."

V'sair turned to him. "But you must, because Lothen will poison this planet as he did his own. Your own future is compromised."

"We will outlast them," Ovie said firmly. "Welks always do. Your civilizations come and go. We shall be safe if we stay here away from you and your segregations."

"Is that not segregation, too?" The red ball purred. "The Plantans are capable of coming here. Once they deplete the land, they will ruin the sea." Ozre's voice cut through the tense silence.

"I think he may be right, Father. I have watched them. They do not respect land, so why should they respect the sea?"

"I don't know what to do." He looked at the glowing blue ball. "Ereth, I don't know what to do."

"Nothing happens by chance. It is all preplanned. Eons ago, your ancestors were dropped here to thrive under the Hixom Sea. The Quyroos were given the land and the Darracians the sky. What is so hard for you to understand? The Trivium is whole," Ereth said gravely.

"The Trivium has been out of balance for too long. The Trivium must be united. One without the other is not whole. One without the other is nothing," Ozre finished the thought.

"Where is Ine?" the girl asked but was ignored.

"Ovie, don't you see? You are the water. The Quyroos are the land, and the Darracians are the air. If the planet is united, the Trivium will be united," V'sair said, his face filled with excitement. "You said this was preplanned?" He turned to the red ball. "All of this was supposed to happen?" His hair hung around his face and to Ovie he looked like nothing more than a boy. Yet Ovie trusted him.

"Nothing happens by accident." Ozre spun around the room. "You have to learn."

"Learn what?" V'sair asked.

"V'sair, V'sair..." Ozre sighed. "If we tell you, what would be the fun for us in that? To learn, you must experience it and come to reason yourself. Don't you remember the Fireblade?"

"All the death, the fighting," V'sair thought feverishly. "The purpose. It was all a waste!" he accused aloud.

"You told me he was bright," Ereth commented as he came to the spot next to Ozre.

"V'sair," Ozre said. "Can't you do any better than that?"

"I don't believe this," Ovie stated.

"I still don't see Ine," Hennith complained.

"You didn't see me, yet I am here," Ozre told her. "Think V'sair."

"It's all for nothing." V'sair looked straight into the warm light of the orb. "All of it. It's all nonsense. Pride, feeling superior, different species. In the end, we are all the same. We build artificial difference and live and die from them."

"Bravo!" Ereth bounced around the room. "One cannot exist without the other."

"It's the basic tenet of our creed and the chanters have it all wrong," V'sair said in a shocked whisper. "No one species is better than the other."

"Ereth, what say you?" Ovie dropped to his knees, his hands clasped before the giant rock wall.

"I manifested in the rock, the waterfall, just as Ozre was in the volcano. We don't need to be represented thusly anymore. True belief makes it possible for you to look inside yourself instead of a prop to understand the meaning of life."

"Is it all an illusion?" Ovie asked.

"If you accept the belief, the illusion is over," Ereth said gently.

"Like the Fireblade. We invested it with false powers," V'sair offered helpfully.

"Oh the power was there," Ozre responded, cruising over to V'sair. He glided along the young man's chest, coming to rest above his heart. "The power was always there. You were just looking in the wrong place."

"We have no choice," Hennith said. "We have to leave here."

"The Elements have spoken," Ovie intoned.

"The Elements have made it so," V'sair finished.

The lights went out sending them into complete darkness. Hennith started to says something, and V'sair silenced her. "Shhhh."

The air cooled, and V'sair saw his breath form in clouds before his mouth. Water dripped, pooling around his feet. He jumped back, losing his balance, bumping into Ovie. The older man steadied him, as the Element relit the room with a blue glow. Their eyes were drawn to the hard-packed floor where the puddle of water swirled, bubbling violently. Ozre hovered over it, warming it with a red heat. V'sair saw an unmistakable shape forming. Pebbles molded, the dull red turning into the shining gold of fire. The rocky quartz buried in the ground melted into a cross-shaped hilt, and the clear handle filled with elements of the soil. V'sair stared in wonder at the stunning Fireblade. He had never seen one as beautiful in his life. Made from the same substance of the very planet, V'sair knew it was for him and the destiny of his home.

"Yes, V'sair." He heard his father's voice. "You are the new Darracia, my son. You have the heart and strength of a warrior but the soul of a leader. Go and fulfill the promise of your purpose. Make Darracia and her people whole."

V'sair kneeled, tears streaming from his eyes. At last, a Fireblade. Hewn from the red earth of Darracia, solely for him. He had achieved his own heart's desire. He was one with the Fireblade. He reached down his strong fingers, digging it out, holding the glowing blade to his face. The heat warmed him, illuminating his face.

Ovie gasped; Hennith's eyes opened wide. The Fireblade's light grew until V'sair was completely encased. His skin turned golden, flames lit his eyes internally. V'sair the heir to the Fireblade was one with the sword as no one else before him. His core belief defined the Fireblade instead of the other way around. His destiny dazzled from the light of power shining from his chest.

Chapter 14

The mauve cliffs of Bina were a sight beyond any description. The jutted out into space, the atmosphere at this height, the craggy graphen bushes growing between the cracks in the rocks. The prisoners were lined up, waiting to be harnessed to the high cranes that rose a mile above the cliffs by slow moving Plantan guards. Given a tasteless soup for breakfast, they marched for hours to roast in the thin air in the mountaintops of Bina. Quyroos had it the worst. Used to the moist, humid air of the Desa, many died where they waited, their lungs exhausted from weak air. Gasping, they would fall to the ground, trembling like fish out of water, until the lack of usable air finished them off. No one could help them; the guards wouldn't allow it. Reminda watched helplessly as a Darracian was thrown from the cliff for stopping to help a dying comrade. His screams went on forever, echoing back from the bottomless fall.

The harness hurt. She was tied into it and thrown over the cliff to free fall for almost a half hour. Reminda was warned not to lose her collection sack, else she be released to fall to her doom. Marek nodded as he went over the cliff before her, and she felt his steady gaze watching her as she dropped. She tried hard not to be afraid. But fear lodged itself in her heart, and she was breathless for most of the drop, the lack of support leaving her disoriented. For a minute, she prayed the rope would break, allowing her to join Drakko and V'sair. But despite her loss, the spirit within her prevailed, and she held onto life as the rope slid through her fingers. Much as Reminda thought about death, she knew she had a job. Marek and the people on Bina needed her. She was the lodestone, the beacon of their hope, and she had to finish her purpose. The queen watched the rock speed past her. The screams of others as they descended filled the air. Buffeted by the hot, dry winds, she called out to the Elements to guide her. Abruptly, her rope ended, and Reminda smashed into the rock wall, scraping her arms raw. Marek was thrown a minute later, seconds behind her. Soon he was beside her, steadying her with soothing words. His entire cheek bled, and Reminda reached up to brush the pebbles embedded in his gray skin. He hissed at the pain, and she shushed him.

They swung free, their legs dangling, the dual suns beating down without mercy. He squinted from the harsh rays of the suns. The sky was a pale green, the soil a crusty white—bone-dry dirt that sucked the moisture from their bones. The air was so thin, so lacking in moisture, that their tongues felt thick, and it hurt to swallow. Marek had a tube of water that he removed from his plaquet. "Drink it slow, and don't let the guards see it," he warned, handing it to Reminda.

"I can't take this. What about the others?"

"We are used to it," he said harshly. "Do not be foolish or brave. Your people need you, their queen, not a martyr."

Reminda bowed her head. "Never think that I…"

Market touched her wrist, sending sparks where their skin touched. "I know, Minda. There is not a soldier here that wouldn't give his or her life for you. I would give my life for you."

Marek was abruptly pulled away to swing dangerously over the vast chasm. Reminda gasped with worry as he spun out into nothingness. He was warned by a staccato voice ordering him to do what he was supposed to do and not hang around. The Plantan guards never tired of this joke, and it had the same uproarious effect on them.

Marek swung forward, grabbing the teal-colored roots of a graphen bush. It had blue blossoms, giving off a sickly sweet smell. He plucked one, sticky white sap coating his fingers.

"Graphen." He showed her. "Put as many in you bag as you can. If you don't bring enough…Arrrr…" He shoved her out of the way as a screaming Quyroo dropped heavily next to them. His line snapped, and his scream continued for a long time. Reminda's eyes followed his drop, the way down seemingly endless.

"Marek…" She touched his arm. "We have to get out of here."

"Of that I have no doubt. We are working on an uprising," he whispered back.

"How? You are unarmed?" she told him.

Marek held up the blossom, twirling it in his fingers. "Perhaps not, your Majesty."

Chapter 15

Zayden sat in the hut, while Bobbien placed a plate of steaming food before him. "Eat, eat, you must. Make up for all those starving days, you must." She smiled at him. He was clean-shaven, and she longed to tweak his cheek as she had done when he was a boy. He had bathed, found new clothes, and looked more like Drakko's son once again. Bobbien was happy. Her heart beat lightly once more in her chest. She discovered on one of her forays into the marketplace that Tulani was in a cell under Seren's guard. She was on Darracia, and she was alive. Bobbien had a message from the castle, from the female Naje, and a plan had formed in her mind to rescue her granddaughter. Now she had to get Zayden well enough to do his part. He had worked with the elders of the community formulating a plan. The attack was for tomorrow.

The food smelled delicious. Zayden had a Quyroo nursemaid in his youth, and the vegetable mash brought back sentimental memories of his time in his father's royal nursery. The odors wafted up, and saliva gathered in his mouth. He could smell the orange Zacky roots mixed with nectar from the wysbie nests. Leaning down, he allowed the steam to bathe his face, his eyelids prickling with emotion. He knew the plate was a beautiful symphony of colors. He smelled the rich humus of the forest, the dense moisture of life. His didn't need his eyes to know it was filled with the yellows, greens, and reds of the Desa, savory with a wealth of flavors. He was hungry, he thought with surprise. He looked up, reaching across the table to touch Denita's soft face. She gasped and pulled away, but he stayed her, the calloused pads of his fingers caressing her cheeks. With the barest touch, his fingers feathered across the planes and angles of her face. He sat back abruptly, calling out, "Bobbien!"

"Aye." The older female lumbered by, her hands on his hips. Zayden reached up, his hands unerring, clasping the fine bones of the old woman's wrists.

"You can see everything now; yep, you can," she told him with a nod.

Zayden sat back pushing the plate away. "You are starving," he stated plainly.

"Aye," Bobbien responded. "We are."

"Why haven't you said anything?" He stood to pace the room, his tongue clicking so that he managed the small space expertly.

"We have." Bobbien was packing a small bag with birthing tools.

Zayden turned to face her, his head cocked. "When?"

"Too drunk, you were to notice."

Denita rose to take his hand, kissing his palm. "You can see all this?"

He pulled her close, resting his chin on the top of his head. "One does not have to be blind not to see."

"But..." Denita was puzzled.

"Eyes are only one of the senses," Bobbien said. "Others, he has. Knows what must be done, he does. Don't waste the food, young 'uns." Bobbien walked out of the hut, leaving them, the sack thrown over her shoulder. "He knows what need to be done," she added.

"Where are you going, Bobbien?" Zayden called out. "You know we plan to attack tomorrow."

"I have a job that must be done. Be back by daylight, I will." She took her traveling staff and left the hut.

"Bobbien," Zayden said, "we go whether you are here or not."

Bobbien nodded, tucking her head under a robe. "Great Sradda willing," was her reply.

Denita reached up to cup his face in her hands. "I have missed you."

Zayden pulled away. "I am no good for you, Denita."

Denita crouched before him, cupping his face in her hands. "You think I care about a paltry thing like sight. I love you, Zayden. I love all of you."

"I am useless."

"You move as well as someone with full sight," Denita responded.

Zayden winced. "I have found a solution, so I can fight and do what my father would have expected. I can't do anything for you."

Denita sighed, "Zayden, I am broken. I may be able to see, but my heart is not like anyone else's. I will never be soft and sweet like some of the women here. I am not kind."

"Don't talk stupid. You are brave and loyal." He turned to her, taking her hand. "I would have died without you. Twice!"

"You could love someone like me?" she asked incredulously.

Zayden stroked her cheek, "You have to ask?" he whispered.

"So why do you hold yourself at a different standard? We are all broken in one way or another. You may not be able to see my face, but you can heal my heart."

"It…it doesn't bother you that I am blind."

"Stupid, stupid warrior. I don't care. I don't care at all."

Zayden covered her mouth with his own. She smelled of sunshine and grass. He rubbed his cheek against her hair, releasing a perfume he identified only with Denita. Pulling her tightly against him, his body tingled as she arched against him, her sighs filling him with excited joy. He held her hands high above them, palm to palm, his voice low "I love you, Denita. I think I have loved you from the minute I first met you."

"Well, why didn't you say so?" Denita kissed him tenderly, stroking the hair from his face.

"I say before the Elements, we are one. Say it with me, Denita," Zayden urged her.

He kissed her deeply, robbing her of breath, but she whispered, "You would make me your own?"

"I will never have my sight?"

"But you will always have my heart." She gripped his hand, placing it on her chest. He moved her mouth to his palm, kissing him. "I love you, Zayden. We are one."

"We are one," he repeated the words, making her his wife.

Denita ripped at his shirt, freeing it from his pants, so that she could caress the hard planes of his chest.

He pulled her into the sleeping quarters, lay down beside her on the low cot, loving her with his hands, his skin, his senses, seeing her like no other woman. He knew her body as if it was part of his own, the skin becoming one. He covered her, thrilling in her cries of delight. Zayden smelled love, tasted love, felt love. He didn't need to see it to know it was there.

Chapter 16

The pains came with daybreak. Naje bent in half as her belly contracted. She had thought it was early. She hadn't expected the child this soon. The midwife, an old Quyroo, rested her palms on her stomach, giving her a knowing look. Her cool hands stroked the woman's taut stomach, massaging the infant within.

"You came," Naje said. She was alone with the Quyroo. Naje had sent all of her women from the room.

"Asked, you did. There is a problem, my lady. The child is breech." Bobbien stood, her eyes locked on Naje's, making sure the pregnant woman understood.

Naje's face turned white. "You can help me?" she asked shrilly.

"Impossible it is not. Just difficult." Bobbien held up her hands. "My hands are old. They are no longer nimble. Turn the child, we must. My granddaughter is imprisoned by Seren. She will be able to do it."

"I can't do that. Seren is overlord of the Desa. He answers only to Lothen."

"Then tell Lothen to turn the child." Bobbien began to pack her tools. "Help you, I cannot."

"No!" Naje held out a hand in supplication. "Don't leave me."

"Deliver your child, I will, but not before you give me back mine."

"I don't have any say on the planet. I don't know if I can get word to Seren."

"You got word to *me*." Bobbien walked toward the door.

"No, wait!" Naje called out to her. "I need you." She held out her caramel hand, imploring the older woman.

"Aye, you do." Bobbien pointed to her belly. "The child must be turned." She looked at Naje directly in the eyes. "You will get my granddaughter released, or I will not help you."

Naje winced. There was a rush of fluid between her legs as the water protecting the baby gushed out.

"The child comes." Bobbien nodded knowingly, pushing her long braids from her face proudly.

She had contacted the old woman, afraid of the Plantan doctor. His cold, blue hands repulsed her. He had forbidden her to eat certain fruits, be outside, and twice he had tried to bleed her as was their custom. It was not right; Naje felt it in her heart it was not the right thing to do.

"It is early," Naje told her. "The child is a month too soon."

"I think not, my lady."

They heard a commotion outside the door. Naje gestured for the Quyroo to hide. She ducked into the closet, leaving the door slightly ajar so she could hear the conversation.

Lothen stalked into the room. "You asked for me? What do you want?"

"The future king begs to be born." Naje gingerly sat on the edge of the bed, her head bowed with another contraction.

"Why are you alone?" He paced the room impatiently. "Where are your women?"

"I don't want them. You must do something for me, Lothen," She implored, her hands clasped.

"She is not alone." Staf Nuen walked in. "I am here."

The two men stared at each other like feral jasts.

"I wasn't talking about you," Lothen sneered. "Where is the doctor?"

"I don't want the doctor. I will have a woman."

"Who?" Staf demanded.

"I want the one called Tulani."

"No." Staf shook his head. "I will bring a Darracian healer."

"By Geva's heart you will not," Naje hissed. She moaned, bending in half. "I want the Quyroo girl!" she wailed. Her hands went to her hair, pulling the long tresses free, and the brown locks cascaded down her back. She looked wild, her eyes glazed white. Her voice took on a husky sound, filling the room, and the voice of Geva filled the chamber.

"She will have the girl, now!" it screamed, a blast of air rushing through the room, scattering papers and clothing.

Lothen stood, his blue face ashen. "By your command, my goddess." He bowed deeply, backing out of the door. "Thy will be done. Deliver the future king safely."

Lothen left the room to do Geva's bidding. Staf looked suspiciously around, then stalked out the door.

"Neatly done." The old Quyroo slid out from her hiding place.

"You will have your child, and I will have mine."

Bobbien nodded regally.

Chapter 17

"Release Tulani!" Seren crushed the note in his fist. "No!"

"You have no choice. You have been commanded."

"By whom. Staf Nuen? He is nothing." Seren wrote furiously at his desk. He handed it to a messenger at his door. "Give that to the king."

Jokin stalked to the door, snatching the note from the servant. "No! Wait here." He pushed him into the hall, turning to round on his son. "Fool! Have you no idea how the court works? What do you care for the girl? Make a trade." He poked him with a red finger.

"But she's our bait. How will we get Bobbien if we let her go?"

"We will follow her," Jokin responded. "She will lead us to them."

Tulani rubbed the raw skin of her wrists as she was lead to a shuttle to take her to the castle. It was shorter trip, she noticed, the fortress hovered below the clouds, not far from the surface of the higher ground of the planet. Bright moonlight lit the night, and she raised her face to catch the light rain drenching them. It misted against her skin, making her close her eyes to revel in the clean feel of the water. It smelled like ozone, and she turned to see the hulking shadow of Aqin in the distance. The sky was dark, the faint outline of the cityscape blurred, the lights mere smudges in the night sky. She scanned the city, noticing that some of the important landmarks—buildings that were built when the city was first sent into the sky, were missing. She searched the floating edifices, but couldn't find the outlines. Statues, signs, anything not associated with one of the larger structures were gone.

The city looked deserted, and Tulani shivered, despite the warmth of the evening.

She traveled in a shuttle in such a state of disrepair that they stalled twice, falling rapidly into frightening tailspins. Finally, she was delivered, shaken, to the doors of the fortress. A Darracian servant informed her she was to follow him. The walked in sullen silence. The great halls were deserted. Rodents left droppings on the once pristine floors. Lights were dim, as if there was not enough power to go around. The busy noise that made Syos a grand capital was gone, leaving the city as a weak shadow of itself. She recognized the way to the Ambros rooms, Reminda's old salon, and felt her heart contract with sorrow. Everyone was gone; the ghosts didn't even walk the halls.

The door opened, and her wrist was grabbed by a hooded servant. Tulani's breath hitched, the realization that the fingers were both dearly familiar and in a shade of red that made her feel faint with relief. Strong arms, and Bobbien's ample chest surrounded the shocked girl—words too difficult to even utter. Tulani rested her head on her grandmother, so overcome that she gulped air, dry sobs wracking her slender body. Bobbien patted her back with a familiarity that brought more tears to her eyes.

"Oh, Grandeam, I thought I'd never see you again."

"Never say so, Tulani. Desert you, I never would. We will have a victory yet. Did he hurt you?" Bobbien searched the young face worriedly.

Tulani shook her head. "No. I think he was using me for bait to bring you in. What are you doing here? It is not safe." Tulani looked up, her star-shaped eyes shining. A feral scream rent the air, making Tulani jump. Bobbien turned to the divan to see Naje's face contorted with pain.

"I made a deal; your small hands I have need of."

She led the girl to the bed. "Help you, my granddaughter." She turned to Tulani. "The baby is breech. Turn it you must."

"How?"

"Inside." Bobbien said grimly.

Tulani shook her head. "I cannot." The woman on the bed was breathing in short pants. Sweat gleamed on her caramel face. Her almond eyes narrowed to slits. "Help me, old woman!" she gasped between pains.

"Easy it is." Bobbien held up her hand, showing her the movements. "Like so…" She rotated her fingers on Tulani's fist, showing her how to turn the child. Bobbien made her cleanse then oil her hands thoroughly.

"Why do you wait?" Naje wailed.

"You want to die from an infection. Do not you know even the most basic rules?" Bobbien asked.

"I. Don't. Care," Naje responded between grunts.

Tulani observed that she was beautiful, despite the strain reddening her face. The veins stood out on her long neck as she groaned. They heard a knock at the door, followed by a harsh voice. Tulani froze, her face ashen, recognizing Staf Nuen's sinister voice.

"What is happening in there?" he shouted, frustrated with the lack of response. "Let me in. I want to see my son."

"Tell him you cannot. She labors and the child comes," Bobbien urged her granddaughter to speak. "Tulani, he knows you are here, but he cannot know that I am."

Tulani swallowed, repeating what her grandmother told her. The door rattled, and this time Naje screamed. "Go away you old fool. Leave me to woman's business!"

Tulani placed herself between the woman's legs. Concentrating, she reached into the tight flesh, feeling the contractions pulse against her hands. She bit her lips against the pain. Bobbien wiped the woman's head, urging her to pant. Tulani felt a blockage, realizing with a start it was the smooth skin of the infant. Her fingers caressed the back of the child, finding a slippery place to squeeze her hands in the narrow opening to adjust the baby. Naje was cursing, her face mottled, blood pouring out of her. Tulani looked up in panic to see her grandmother's gentle eyes smiling.

"Normal, this is. Don't worry. Let the Elements guide your hand, girl."

Tulani bit her lip, relaxing her hands, feeling moving them carefully to ease them between the baby and the woman's womb. She found an opening, slipping them to surround the baby, turning him ever so gently. Naje was shrieking like a banshee, her face mottled. Tulani looked worriedly at her grandmother, who smiled benignly.

"Good work, you do, young healer," Bobbien told her proudly.

"I see his head!" Tulani face lit with relief. The baby's head crowned in the opening. "He is coming," Tulani said with awe.

"Push now, my lady. Don't be afraid. Push!" Bobbien told Naje as she wiped her head.

Naje gritted her teeth, concentrating all her effort on pushing the baby out. She groaned a sound so deep, it came from the well of her womb.

"I have his head," Tulani shouted, her face filled with joy. This was beautiful, and it made her feel happy.

Another push and the shoulders burst through, followed by the rush as the feet escaped.

"My son," Naje asked urgently, "is he well? I don't hear him."

Bobbien grabbed the child, slapping him heartily, hearing the wails of life fill the room. Tulani's smile faded as Bobbien rested the infant on his mother's breast.

"Great Sradda, Grandeam, did you see…"

"Quiet! Be still," Bobbien warned her as she finished the job, cleaning the new mother.

Naje looked up, her eyes filled with gratitude and just a bit of surprise.

"So, you were right old woman. He was not early." She played thoughtfully with the child's tiny hand.

"Just as I thought."

Staf banged on the door. "Let me in, Naje! Now!"

"All right, you will be?" Bobbien asked, ignoring the racket.

Naje shrugged indifferently. "You had better leave. Take the girl and leave." She looked down at the infant, smiling.

"Swaddle him first, I think." Bobbien wrapped the baby tightly in blankets.

Bobbien turned, grabbing Tulani's hand as if she were a child, escaping out of the chambers through the rear terrace. Reaching into her bag, she pulled out a large robe. "Now I will swaddle you," she said with a smile. "Put this on, girl." she said as she covered her own braids with the cowl like hood. They jumped over the balustrade to leap down the many levels until they could descend to the vehicle station to fly home in a stolen shuttle.

Naje looked up as both Lothen and Staf entered the room, the baby wrapped tightly in swaddling.

"A son?" Staf asked.

Naje smiled, her carmine lips wide. "A son for Darracia."

Staf reached out to take his son's hand. The webbed fist grabbed the gray finger tightly. Staf growled in shock. Flicking back the blanket, he stared in horror at a blue infant with a shock of white hair. Lothen threw back his head and roared with laughter.

Chapter 18

Zayden used a long staff as a weapon as he stood in front of a group of Quyroos. A volunteer faced him, defensively backing as Zayden lunged with the stick. He tapped him on the shoulder, despite the Quyroo's nimble feet. The observers clapped in wonder as Zayden showed them moves to protect themselves in an offense.

To anyone who didn't know him, they would think he was fully sighted. But for the quiet clicking of his tongue, he seemed a great warrior. Denita watched from under the janjan tree, proud of her man's fleet footwork.

Zayden invited three men up. The land was marshy, the light rain falling but ignored by the combatants. They had made a clearing, cutting the low-hanging branches, so they could practice fighting skills. Most were amazed with the blind warrior's skill. No matter how quiet they were, he heard them approach, using a stick to show the movements to dispatch an enemy. Placing himself in the middle, they arranged an attack, surprised by his deft movements. They were dispatched without harm, and Zayden lined them up again for another go. This time, they managed to outwit his moves, and Zayden applauded their movements. His easy smile instilled confidence, and soon his group had swelled to hundreds. He worked with them all day, teaching them defensive movements.

Cosfar stormed over, his red face seething. "You play soldier with a blind man! To what purpose?"

Zayden reached down, taking a cloth to wipe the perspiration running down his face and neck.

"You have a problem, Cosfar?" He asked.

"Yes! This is madness. Madness. How do you expect them to go up against the Plantans tomorrow? With sticks." He gestured the staff. "They have guns."

Zayden nodded. "You are right. So should we stay here like herns, waiting for them to find us and pick us off one by one?"

The crowd rumbled in agreement.

Cosfar turned, "You listen to a blind man. A Darracian? You would trust one such as him?"

He spun to hit Zayden, who bent backward, Cosfar's fist flying past him uselessly.

"He is not blind anymore," Denita called out. "He has sight." Denita ran to their small hut, coming back a minute later, her hands hidden behind her back.

"You lie," Cosfar hissed.

Denita called out "Zayden!" and pitched something at him. He caught it easily, his hand wrapping around the hilt of his Fireblade.

The small clearing got deathly quiet.

"Denita…" Zayden held out the sword for her. "Where did you get it?"

"I've always had it. It was on your ship. I never let it out of my sight." She had been saving it for the right time to give it back to him.

"I don't…I don't know…"

"Try, Zayden. Just try."

Holding the Fireblade with two hands, Zayden closed his eyes. His fingers gripped the hilt, and the sword leaped in his hands, the familiar hum singing out in triumph.

Zayden swallowed convulsively, sweat beading his brow. His muscled arms quivered, his knuckles white.

"Tell me the color," he whispered, then spoke loudly. "Denita, tell me the color."

"Blue, my warrior. You blade is bright blue with the color of justice." She turned to the crowd of Quyroos. "Will you follow him?"

"Aye!" A large male called out, raising his pike in the air. "I will join him to defeat the Plantans."

"Me too!" Another jumped up. Soon the air was filled with the cries of the Quyroos, united in the support of a new leader.

"He is blind, you fools. He is blind!" Cosfar's shouts were smothered by the growing crowd surrounding Zayden.

"We march!" Zayden raised his shining blade into the air. "We march to retake our home."

His small army roared with approval, forming lines to follow the glowing beacon of justice to their destiny.

Chapter 19

The weak boy was on his stomach reaching under the bunk for the coins he had thrown there. Unis eyed him with a nasty smile. He had sent the others to race around the compound, leaving him time alone with the big Darracian's squire. There had been a showdown. It had been weeks in coming. Unis antagonized Marek, wanting to separate the protective Darracian from his little squire. The little one intrigued him, and Unis wanted to get to the bottom of those long-lashed eyes. He set Marek up for a fight, punishment being a run around the track of the compound for the whole night with the rest of the Darracians from his quarters. The entire barrack was sent out for the senseless exercise, save the young boy. Marek hesitated, not wanting to follow the orders, but Reminda urged him not to disobey. Unis threw contraband coins to roll on the floor, then ordered the weakling to retrieve them.

Every time he bent over, Unis pressed his baton into the fleshy part of the boy's thigh, delighting in the squeak he made when it zapped him. Unis laughed, his head thrown back in mirth. He was so bored on Bina. He rolled a handful of pebbles under the heating units, chuckling gleefully as Reminda crawled on all fours to retrieve them. Unis came close so that when Reminda turned to find him breathing heavily on the back of her neck, she turned. Reminda could count the ugly pores on his rubbery nose. He stared at her feminine face.

"Who are you?" Unis whispered as licked his lips, frozen with the realization that Reminda was not a boy.

She used this advantage to smile coyly, swallowing down bile, peeping up at him through softened eyes. Reaching out, she squeezed his upper arm and sighed dramatically. "You are so very strong," she told him coyly.

Unis gulped. "You are female."

"Oh, please don't tell," came the sweet reply. She moved closer to his face and spoke in a seductive voice. "I just want to be close to you." She shivered, closing her eyes dreamily.

"I don't know. It's against the rules. I could get in trouble. I should report this." He looked out the window warily at the running males, gaging how much time he had.

"Can't it be our little secret? If you tell, they will move me to the women's side, and I'll never see you." Reminda moistened her lips, leaning forward to kiss him gently. She brushed her breast against his arm as she leaned in. Unis reached over to grab her, but the loud squawk of his communication device made him jump back guiltily. His commander's tinny voice came through, slicing the tense air. "Unis!" he shouted. "Unis, report to me at once!"

Unis stood shakily, bumping into a chair dazedly. He stumbled out the door, leaving it wide open, allowing the freezing morning air to enter. The prisoners filed in, Marek's worried gaze finding Reminda with relief. She sat on the floor, a satisfied smile on her face.

"Are you well?" he asked, his face filled with concern.

Reminda reached behind her to take out a baton. "I think we have our catalyst," she told him with a smile.

Marek took the weapon, considering it thoughtfully. He looked up at Reminda.

"I distracted him, but he knows I am female. We must do it today."

Marek nodded grimly. "Yes, today."

Chapter 20

Zayden's forces swelled. Male and females with makeshift weapons marched through the Eastern Provinces, picking up more and more Quyroos as they traveled into the swampy fells, tramping with the single-minded purpose of taking out the oppressive rule.

They used whatever tools they could find from the land. A young boy approached Zayden eagerly, pulling at his tunic.

"Are you the commander?" he asked.

Zayden kept walking. "Go back to your mother, little boy. Only adults can fight."

"I can help!"

Zayden nodded. "Of that I'm sure. Go back and watch the young 'uns, freeing up the elders."

The boy held up something in Zayden's line of vision. "What! Are you blind? Look I have something that will help!"

Zayden paused, causing the whole crowd to slow, a hush falling over the mob.

The boy realized Zayden was indeed sightless. "I'm sorry, my lord," he said in a shocked whisper. He placed a stick with hollowed-out gourds attached with vines in Zayden's hand. "Look. I made this weapon. We all did. We have been annoying the Plantans and doing some damage to their convoys. We are not afraid to fight" He gestured to a small tribe of children, each holding a handful of the slingshots.

"You don't need skill. Look," he then amended. "I mean listen." The boy loaded the gourd with a rock. "Name a target."

Denita stepped forward. "Can you hit the Wysbie nest on that tree?" The boy looked at her with apprehension. "Oh, they're gone," she said. "Can't you see the nest is empty? Unless it's too far?"

The boy spun the gourds in his agile hands, so fast they became an orange blur. Zayden cocked his head, listening to the whir of the weapon, followed by the whistle of the small rock launched to bring down the nest. Zayden didn't need to hear the crowd's murmur of approval to know it hit the target true.

"How many of these do you have?"

"We have hundreds of them. We have been preparing for an attack."

Cosfar stomped over, his face a red mask of rage. "Stupid boy," he sneered. "They have no skill to lob mere rocks at the enemy. Go back to your mother and hide until it is over."

"No," Zayden told him. "Think Cosfar of the effect if hundreds of these missiles are launched at once."

"Don't forget the Zandy grenades!" Denita held one of the homemade bombs in her hands.

"You will all die!" Cosfar warned. "You fight the Darracians as well as the Plantans!"

"Then either way we will die! Whether it is in battle or on a transport to Sradda know where, we have no choice. I believe that when my kinsmen realize their freedom lies united with us, we will see a defection."

"You don't know that," Cosfar replied.

"That is true. One thing I do know is that the Elements taught us that only when they unite, they create the perfect balance of life." He raised his voice for all to hear. "My father, King Drakko, died for his belief that every member of this planet must be equal and deserves a voice. Maybe we have to follow the Elements example and unite as well."

Cosfar silently considered this idea.

"Who wants one of these?" Zayden held up the slingshot.

There was a chorus of "ayes." Cosfar picked one up, tucking it in his loincloth. Denita looked at him with a question. He glanced at Zayden, admiration in his eyes, and said, "Perhaps, I have been the one who was blind."

Chapter 21

V'sair set up a command center in Ovie's living space. Ovie invited the clan leaders of each of the families to help formulate a plan to invade Darracia. They arrived wet and exhausted, from a network of caves that ran under the seabed. At first, they refused to join him, but when Ovie recounted his experience with the Elements, they agreed, but with many differences of opinion.

"This is foolhardy, V'sair." Ovie pointed to a map spread out across a table.

"I don't see another way. A frontal attack, to take out the village on the Plains of Dawid."

"Just march out of the water and attack?" Pudar, an elder, asked. "No disrespect, young man, but they will wipe us out. I would rather take my chance staying down here until they all kill each other off. Aside from that," he added, "how will we prevent being mistaken for Plantans? The resemblance is remarkable."

V'sair nodded. "You don't have facial tattoos. All of them are marked at puberty. It's the lack of the design that gives you away as different."

"Still, it seems foolish to make war when they are not even aware of our existence," another one of the elders spoke up. "They are strong, warlike; we are not."

There was a great murmuring of approval. V'sair ran a hand through his loose hair. He refused to braid it until he returned home. The girl Hennith spoke up, "No, don't you see there are so many of us? Their forces are limited."

V'sair turned to her. "Exactly how many of your species are capable of fighting?"

"We number in the thousands. I have heard that there is a finite number of Plantans. The worry is of the Darracians. They will sway any battle."

"It still doesn't matter how many we are. We won't be able to reach the city in the clouds," a tall male interrupted, his face worried.

One of the guards who had brought him to this place spoke. "It won't be as hard as you think. The city is sliding onto the planet. They have used up all the Randam and are running out of fuel."

"How could they use up the crystals?" Ovie asked, his face incredulous.

"When they bombed the Desa, the crystals rotted on the broken trees. They have decimated their work force. V'sair is right. They are sucking the life from this planet, and we will be next."

"If we make a concerted attack, from each of the shorelines, meeting together in the center, we would not only surprise them but overwhelm them with the sheer number," V'sair said, blue finger pointed out the four entry points to land.

Ovie shook his head. "It could work. If we had muster support from the landwalkers, the Plantans would be easily overwhelmed."

A young guard burst into the room, breathlessly interrupting. "It has begun. The Quyroos are marching en masse from the Eastern Provinces, under the leadership of a Darracian."

"This is a sign from the Elements. Do you know who the leader is?" V'sair asked.

"I don't know him. They say he is blind," the guard answered.

"That's crazy, a blind leader," Pudar sputtered. Many agreed loudly.

"Perhaps the Elements are guiding them," Hennith offered.

"It doesn't matter." V'sair shrugged his shoulders as he rolled up the map, looking to Ovie for direction. "If they are heading west, then they are going to attack in the Plains of Dawid. What is our most direct route there?"

"We swim east," Ovie stated. He directed the biggest group to follow them. Three other groups were sent to various shores to meet in the center of the great land mass.

Armed with their spears, V'sair with his blade, they left to join the rebels heading for Plantan territory.

Chapter 22

The line moved painstakingly slow this morning when they reported to work.

It was bitter cold, the coming dawn barely reaching the thin atmosphere of Bina. The bleak landscape blended with the colorless sky. Marek shifted from foot to foot in the cold, trying to block the worst of the winds from Reminda. The queen's eyes teared, making frozen tracks down her tattooed cheeks. Marek reminded her to keep her face down.

Harnesses were cinched, and soon Reminda was free falling over the cliffs, her heart soaring, knowing that whatever the outcome, she was doing something to help the others.

She bounced painfully, feeling the descending drop as the next person came to hang suspended near her territory of bushes. She looked up to see Marek hurtling down, too close to the stone wall. An outcropping of rocks jutted away from the cliff, and Reminda watched in horror as he collided with the mass, a groan escaping his body. Several rocks came loose, falling downward hitting workers on their way to oblivion. He flew past her, his eyes closed in pain, one leg a bloody mess.

Reminda spun herself into a circle, using her feet to propel away from the wall to try and reach him. The suns rays began to burn through her hat to bake her head. Sweat drenched her body, as the temperature radically changed. Her feet dangled, and no matter how hard she pushed herself away from the wall, she couldn't get her straps to lower her. A shout from above made her look up into the blinding rays of the suns.

"Hey you!" a guard shouted, his hands resting on his gun looked down. "Start picking."

A hand touched her back, and she turned, relief warring with worry when she saw Marek painfully making his way up the rock wall. He waved to the guard, showing crushed blossoms in his big hands. They guard shrugged, walking away to check on the other side. Marek made eye contact the men of their barracks. As planned, the soldiers clustered themselves so they all appeared to be picking blossoms. Reminda watched as they formed two layers. The ones closer to the rock wall, chipped away at the surface, while a man behind them covered their bodies with their own as they picked the graphen.

"Are you all right?" she asked Marek.

"I was pushed." Marek responded.

"I thought so. Do you have it?"

Marek nodded, showing her the handle of the baton.

"How long do they have to dig?" Reminda used her pickax to start scraping an opening in the rock face. It crumbling easily; her hands were soon coated with the mauve dust.

"Hard to say. Will you be able to climb up?" Marek studied her face intently.

Reminda looked at the vast wall rising above her. "I must. Great Sradda give me strength."

"Tomo will be right behind you." He nodded to his next in command, who motioned back at him.

"I wish it were you." She placed her hand on his arm. "Will you be able to climb up with that leg?"

"This scratch?" he laughed. "Drakko would make fun of me."

The mention of her dead husband sobered them, and Reminda looked away.

The day wore on, and soon the entire cliff was honeycombed with small pockmarks that were methodically stuffed with crushed graphen blossoms. Every so often the Plantans would look down the cliff wall to see the Darracians and Quyroos working silently in the oppressive heat.

Reminda's tongue swelled in her mouth, the mauve dust clogging her nostrils. She rested her head against the warm stone, exhausted.

"It won't be long now, my lady." Marek came up behind her. He hefted her up from behind. His hands molded to her backside, but no matter how clinical he tried to be, Marek knew where his hands were. And her shaking body told him that Reminda was just as aware. "Start climbing," he ordered.

Reminda stretched her arms to grip small spaces, so she could inch her way up. Her fingernails tore; her hands were scraped raw. She glanced down to see row after row of Darracians and Quyroos swinging to Marek. He used his baton's heated tip to light small rags. They stole looks at her progress, watching Tomo inch up silently behind her.

As planned, the small group of Quyroos started to chant the song the signal that they all had to get ready. Reminda's hand fumbled with the crumbling edge of the cliff. Her arms shook with effort, and she was suddenly afraid she would not be able to make it. She felt a hand push her up so that she lifted over onto the top.

Tomo followed her up and screamed, "Now!" He ran forward, grabbing the guard's gun, spinning him so that he was launched over the side of the cliff. He aimed the gun at a armed Venturian running toward them, his weapon blasting away. Tomo shot him then ran to hit the switches reeling in all the harnessed men and women hanging off the side of the cliff.

Reminda was on the other side, going down the rows of winches reversing the direction, so the air filled with the whine of the machines.

The first explosion rumbled underneath them. Reminda worried that the graphen wasn't going to be dry enough to be an effectual explosive. The staccato of their homemade bombs going off rocked the mountain. Hordes of prisoners bounced onto the hilltop, screaming as they took off to attack the guard's quarters. For a minute, Reminda stared at the horizon, not knowing what to do, when Marek limped up to her. She smiled in relief. He smelled of graphen and looked slightly stoned from breathing all the smoke.

"We have to get out of here. The graphen veins run deep. Once a tree is lit, the flame will burn to the root. I'm not sure, but Bina could be doomed."

"Well, good riddance to that!" Reminda panted as they dodged the crowds.

Marek pulled Reminda along. It was bedlam. Prisoners stormed the guards, making short work of the opposition. Desolate, on the backside of the solar system, Bina was not considered a threat, and Lothen used a small command of barely a dozen men to control it.

Reminda gasped, hiding her face in Marek's strong shoulder, when a Darracian marched past them holding a pike with Unis's head decorating the top of it. Loaded onto the first batch of ships, Reminda watched Bina shrink as they headed back to Darracia, her home and her destiny. An explosion rocked the spaceship as Bina exploded into a million tiny pieces.

"What?' Reminda sat up straighter. "What happened?"

Marek looked down at her fondly, and he took a bold move and kissed the top of her head. "Just as I thought, the graphen roots ran deep. My guess is our small detonations caused a chain reaction."

"Look!" She pointed a long blue finger out the window at the floating rubble. "It's…"

"Gone," Marek finished grimly.

Chapter 23

"Certainly we should head to the Desa, Grandeam," Tulani said breathlessly as they walked toward the marketplace on the Plains of Dawid. "Grandeam!" She pulled at Bobbien's covered arm. "We go to certain death here."

"Cover your braids as I showed you, girl." Grandeam admonished. "Don't walk so fast. A job we have yet to do."

"What could we possibly do?" She looked around into the sea of Darracian faces. Hardly any Quyroos were left. You could count them on your hand. Bobbien strategically placed her staff behind her so it looked like a Darracian tail. She had done the same for her granddaughter. They were draped in voluminous robes, worn by Darracian healers. Cowls hid their faces and braids. They walked down the narrow lanes, hawkers calling out illegal items. This was not the home Tulani remembered. It looked lawless—the pinched, hungry faces of the Darracians testimony that it was not the same planet for them as well. No longer privileged, they scrambled on the surface trying to feed whatever family members they could. Tulani looked at their faces, seeing a princess here, a countess there, men noticeably missing. Clothes looked worn, colorless, frayed. Many children looking emaciated, as if hunger as well as fear was their companion.

"Ozre," she murmured, "what have you allowed?"

Her grandmother overheard her, said simply, "Only man allows. Elements are bystanders. A message I must get to a few merchants. Watch for soldiers."

Bobbien walked through the maze as if she'd done it a thousand times. She stopped, pulling a stall merchant close, whispering a short message. Tulani stood behind her, her eyes scanning the marketplace for trouble.

She watched her grandmother lean in, her red fingers wrapping around the gray wrists. There were nods of understanding. Sometimes she heard a nervous gasp, but always the reaction was swift. The key people were chosen to get the message, and slowly, one by one, stalls shut down. Then the crowd dissipated, and Tulani yearned for the moment that she and her grandmother could melt into the red of the forest.

They emerged from a filthy alleyway to head for the forest, when a white stallius mounted by a Quyroo stood in their way. Tulani shuddered as she recognized both the animal and the man who rode it. The soldier was surrounded by warriors who blocked their path.

"Who are you?" the officer demanded.

Tulani felt her muscles quiver with fear, her jaw clench with hatred. Before she could answer, she was grabbed by strong hands on either side, and the cowl was ripped from her head. Bright sunlight blinded her, but she was held fast by her captors.

"Ah, Tulani." Seren laughed. "I have missed you. We never got to finish what we started. Take them!" he ordered, spinning quickly to gallop toward his command hut.

She was back in the prison in the basement. Bobbien was missing; she worried mightily. The heavy metal door opened with a squeal, and the old Darracian servant Kovo unlocked the door. He motioned for her to follow him.

"Where are you taking me?" she asked in a hurried whisper.

"Seren wants you to watch what he does with your grandmother," he replied without looking at her face. His shoulders were bent, his steps heavy with defeat.

"Why do you help him?" Tulani demanded. "They are destroying the planet."

"What choice do I have?" the old man shot back. "If I don't cooperate, he will send both my wife and I to Bina. We are too old. Oh how this place has changed," Kovo lamented. "Before the invasion, I was a distributor of machinery. I had wealth, status and many Quyroo servants…" He grew quiet shaking his head. "Oh, how the outlook has changed for me!"

"What do you mean?" Tulani looked at his face in the dark room.

"I was nice to my servants, but I never realized how hard they work. When Drakko, you know, the last king, wanted them to join the Moon Council, I voted against it. I didn't understand how it was for them. I didn't know." He shook his craggy head as he shuffled up another level of steps. "It is not fair."

"No," Tulani agreed quietly. "It is not."

"Everyone should be treated with dignity," Kovo stated.

"Yet you work for Seren. He is not a fair commander."

The Darracian shrugged, much like the Quyroo fashion. "One must eat."

Tulani touched his arm. "You can help me."

He shook his head. "I cannot."

Tulani followed him to the top floor and was led to a door at the end of a long hallway. She entered to find Bobbien strapped to a chair, her head hanging, her braids loosened, hiding her face. Her raspy breath filled the room.

"Grandeam!" Tulani ran to her grandmother, falling to her knees. She touched her leg but got no response.

"She may be close to death." Seren laughed. "She was always a fool. She wouldn't tell me what she was doing in the marketplace."

Tulani touched Bobbien's cheek, relief filling her when the star-shaped eyes winked. Bobbien groaned long and loud, letting everyone in the room know she yet breathed.

"Ah!" Seren smacked a whip against the palm of his hand. "She lives. What to do, what to do…shall I hurt the granddaughter to make the old one talk or hurt the elder to make you tell me what you were doing? So many choices, ha!"

"We were doing nothing!" Tulani shouted. "Nothing. How could you hurt Bobbien?" Tulani accused him, her face angry. "She set your arm when you were seven. What kind of monster have you become?"

Seren stalked over to her, grabbing a fistful of hair, pulling Tulani across the floor. He leaned closer, his face inches from her. "We can finish this once and for all between us, Tulani. Give me what I want, and I will let her go."

Tulani looked at the slack figure of her grandmother in the chair. She glanced out of the window to gaze at the city in the clouds, now listing so heavily to one side that it rested on part of the Desa, crushing whatever trees grew there. The dreams were dead. V'sair was gone. What did anything matter anymore? All she had was Bobbien, and she would do anything to protect her. She noticed it was so quiet outside the air was thick, as though a thunderstorm was coming. Taking a deep breath, she looked up at Seren, her eyes filled with tears, and said, "Tell me what you want."

He leaned down to kiss her roughly, and then the door swung open, Kovo in the portal. He was holding Bobbien's walking stick. "Here girl," he called out, throwing the stick to her. "Defend yourself! We march to take back Darracia! The species have united!" He let out a war whoop and ran from the house.

Tulani reached out, deftly catching the stick in her hands, her agile fingers wrapping around it.

Seren shouted, "What is the meaning…" Tulani spun, her leg landing squarely in Seren's groin, bringing him to his knees. He screamed, fumbling with his holster to grab his gun. Tulani banged his hand with the stick; Seren howled with rage. He stood, then crouched low, running to attack her. Tulani bashed him in the shoulder, knocking him sideways. He rolled to stand to come at her again, but Tulani leaped high, smacking him on the back of the head. Seren fell like a toppled tree, moving no more.

"Tulani…" Bobbien called, her voice weak. "Pull the hair from my eyes. I can't see."

"No time, Grandeam." Tulani fumbled with the knots on the rope. "What do you know that I don't?"

"Has it started? We just had to last until Zayden hits the town. Rescue us, he will."

"Zayden? V'sair's brother?"

"Yes. Attacking, at dawn he is. He has rallied the Quyroos, and I have spoken with the Darracians. We will throw out this yoke of oppression together."

Bobbien stood, leaning heavily on Tulani. They heard fierce shouting from the open window. They both gazed out welcoming the sight of a line of Quyroos walking toward them, the horizon filled with armed warriors.

"Let's get out of here," Tulani urged.

"Put Seren in a place where he'll do the least damage, we will." Bobbien smiled with a big grin.

Chapter 24

Lothen looked helplessly over the balustrade, watching the city sink lower and lower. At this point even the broken contours of Aqin the volcano were higher. Syos hung lopsided, many of the buildings rocked drunkenly on the waves of the Hixom Sea. They were doomed. The planet had been stripped of its resources, just like Planta.

He saw a line of movement from the dark recesses of the red Desa. Like a writhing snake, it moved closer, the dual rays of Rast and Nost illuminating the morning horizon. It had stopped raining, the suns baking the forests so it steamed with heat. Lothen's narrowed eyes watched the small line cresting the final hilltop to the Plains of Dawid, realizing with horror that it was a mass of Quyroos, their marching feet beating in a strange rhythm, as if calling more to join their battalion. Armed with primitive weapons, he counted rows of thousands of them. The sun splashed its brilliance onto the glistening gray water of the Hixom Sea. The dazzling rays pranced on the surface, illuminating a school of blue fish swimming close to the surface. Lothen leaned closer, his eyes starting out of his head when he realized they were not fish, but hundreds of blue arms swimming above the water line. He leaned over, seeing a synchronized swarm of Plantans swimming determinedly to the shoreline. He knew instinctively these were not his people, but who could they be? A lone white-haired head popped above the choppy waves to pause and stare right at him. His eyes locked with his nephew V'sair—alive and with an army swimming behind him. Lothen turned to go inside racing through the hallways, skidding on the slippery polished floors, rounding a corner to dash into the throne room. Staf Nuen sat dejectedly on the throne, his fist under his chin, his leg swung negligently over the arm of the chair. The court was empty. The wind whistled through the hollow room, blowing abandoned papers littering the floor. Lothen stooped to pick one up. "What is the meaning of this?" He scanned the notice, crumbling it after reading the words.

"Primitive, but effective, as you can see," Staf pointed to his vacant room. "A call to arms, for all species. They mean to overthrow us."

"Nuen, Nuen!" Lothen screamed. "We are being attacked. Call out the guards! Go out there and defend our home."

Staf Nuen ignored him, his yellowed eyes narrowed in the dark room.

"Staf!" Lothen grabbed him.

Staf turned slowly, his face feral in the darkness. "I don't care."

"Raise the army. For your son!"

This time Staf Nuen threw back his head to laugh, the bitter sounds bouncing off the walls to echo in the empty room. Staf Nuen laughed like a mad man, spittle foaming at his mouth. Lothen backed out of the room.

Lothen walked purposefully to his staff headquarters, coming into a near deserted chamber. Three Plantan commanders sat at the command table, talking quietly.

"An invasion! A revolution!" Lothen announced, banging his fist on the table.

"We have heard of it." One of his generals stood, twisting his arm ring nervously.

"Where are your men?" He glanced around the table noting not a single newly appointed Darracian was there. "Where?" he screamed, the veins sticking out on his blue neck. His white war knot listed to one side, making him appear as off balanced as he sounded.

"They have deserted. The Darracians are missing. Many of our Plantan warriors have gone missing."

Lothen pulled out his sword, menacing it before their frightened faces. "I expect every able-bodied male—Plantan, Darracian, or Quyroo—to be behind me on those beaches within the hour!"

"Sire, the Quyroos are near extinct, and we have deported them all." A lone general stood, shifting from one foot to the other.

Lothen struck off his head with a single blow. It landed with a bloody thud on the conference table to roll into the center, the surprised, sightless eyes still fluttering.

"Are there any questions?" Lothen asked with menace.

The remaining males jumped up, rushing out of the room. Lothen approached the dead man. Reaching down, he ripped off one of the bracelets adorning the man's upper arm. He worked it up his forearm to his bicep. Flexing his arm, he watched it mold to the muscle and bone of his own arm, the metal snake undulating in its new home.

Lothen ran to the stables, saddled his black stallius himself to leap out of the low fortress and land on the planet. There were no guards, not a single one. He galloped over the spongy ground toward the Plains of Dawid. The humidity made bathed his skin with a sheen of perspiration. He wiped his damp palms down the material of his pants. The tightly woven streets of the marketplace were eerily silent. He walked the stallius though the rutted lanes, the wind picking up to whistle down the narrow alleyway. The animal balked, neighing, her eyes rolling in her skull. She pranced, nearly unseating him. Lothen tugged on the reins, his spurred feet, digging holes into her dark sides. Her coat frothed pink where he jabbed her.

He pulled the reins making his way toward Seren's compound. It had been looted. Clothes lay discarded in the dirt square; broken plates, items from the house were strewn haphazardly around. A door hung drunkenly on its side, half opened. Lothen dismounted, tying his stallius's reins to a post. Taking out his pistol, he walked into the darkened interior. It was deathly quiet, the bang of a loose shutter making Lothen jump. He heard a whimper and walked cautiously toward a pantry door. One hand on the doorknob, he swung it open to find Seren bound and gagged on the floor. His pants had been pulled down around his legs, leaving his red backside exposed for all and sundry.

Lothen pulled him out with an ungentle tug, then sliced off the shackles.

"Pull your pants up!" he commanded. Seren's red face grew pinker as he hastily complied. "Where are your men?"

"Deserted." He cleared his throat.

"Did they do that to you?"

"No, it was Tulani and her grandmother," he replied shamefacedly.

Lothen slammed into the commander's head with his gun. "A girl and an old woman! Where are your men?" he demanded.

"They have run. It is the warrior Zayden. They have heard of him, and he is on the way here!" Sweat shone on his frightened face. The Quyroo shook with terror.

"Get your guns and muster up whoever you can!" Lothen shoved him away. "We fight. Move to the beach."

Chapter 25

The suns beat down to bake the red sands into a pale pink. The heat shimmered so that the distance looked as smudged as a watercolor. Lothen sat on his black stallius, Seren to the right of him on Hother. Both animals snorted, pawing the loose sand. Seren worked hard to control his beast, crushing the wings that threatened to spread against his command. He thought briefly of sending the animal back to the stables for another mount but lacked even one servant to do his bidding. Every man was armed and ready for the impending battle.

The wind picked up, whipping the gray sea into a frenzy of foam. The sky darkened, and Lothen spread his hands wide, while balancing himself on the stallius. "Geva, great goddess of destruction, you must wipe out the Quyroo once and for all."

He looked dusted in gold, his blue skin iridescent with sweat. His arms were covered from shoulder to elbow with snake rings, each a clear message of past victories to his enemies.

The wind screamed, sending sand and rocks flying. A cloud shaped itself in the sky. The oncoming Quyroos slowed, suddenly fearful of the fury of the wind. They paused, cowering on the upper-most ridge before the descent into the Plains of Dawid. The whole valley spread before them in a great, dusty pink bowl, the wind gusting to swirl great gouts of sand into tornadoes dancing along the great open space.

Zayden yelled over the howling wind, "What's the matter with them? Denita, be my eyes."

Denita squinted through the growing darkness. "Lothen has conjured something up, Zayden. Something evil."

"There is no such thing as evil," Zayden scoffed. "Move forward." He motioned with his arm but felt Denita pull his elbow back.

"They are frightened!" she yelled over the growing noise. They held their spot, buffet by the warm winds, their clothes plastered to their bodies in a standoff.

Zayden heard Lothen praying to his dark deity.

"Kill them, Geva!" he commanded.

Clouds roiled in the sky, turning day into the darkest night. A dark ball of energy spun across the sky, whizzing past the Quyroo's heads, making them cringe with fear as they dropped to the ground. A fetid smell followed the ball in a trail of cosmic refuse.

"Tell me what you see!" Zayden shouted to Denita.

"Lothen and his army are between us and the sea. His forces are surprisingly small. If we can get our people to rush down the hill, I think we can take them. Oh…" She stopped talking.

"What?" Zayden reached out to grab her arm. "Something is happening."

"I don't know if this is good or bad…oh no. There are reinforcements coming from the water. A whole army of Plantans is swimming to the shore. Zayden," she said, her voice full of despair, "we are lost. We are a lost cause."

"Shit," Zayden cursed. "Think, think, think…" He hit his forehead with the palm of his hand.

"Hold on!" Denita stopped him. "Lothen…oh Zayden…Lothen is moving to attack his own people. They are different somehow."

"What is different?" Zayden urged, grasping for anything. "Tell me what you see. Leave out no detail," he commanded.

"The tattoos, Zayden. They don't have them. They don't have those war rings on their arms either. They are slighter. I have never seen Plantans without tattoos on their faces."

"They have no tattoos?" Zayden asked in a rush.

Denita shook her head, replying, "I mean, no, and they don't wear their hair in war knots either."

"I don't know who they are, but they are not Plantan." He stood, turning to be seen by his troops. He could sense a difference. More fighters had joined the ranks. His army increased, picking up new members from all over Darracia. He needed to coalesce them into a cohesive fighting force. They were untrained, unprepared, and probably doomed. The one thing they were, he realized with a smile, was united. "There is a battle going on down there. Are we going to sit here like a target, or go down and kick some Plantan ass?" Zayden shouted, standing his full seven-foot height. There were murmurs, a few cheers. He spun around, clicking his tongue to locate his troops. "I may be just a king's bastard, and a blind one at that, but I am willing to go down there and show Lothen and his army what we are made of." The voices stilled, his soldiers watching his every move. Zayden filled his chest and spoke as loud as his voice would carry. "The time has come for us to change or die. All men and women, no matter their species or color, should have the same rights as everyone else. I declare this day, that I will take my father, King Drakko's dream and turn it to reality. As the Elements are the Trivium, so are the species of Darracia. One is not whole without the other. The Trivium is whole, and so are our people. Be they gray, red, or blue—one is not whole without the other. I declare for one and all that the species of Darracia are whole and equal, or nothing at all!" Noise of hundreds of shouts erupted, filling the bowl shape meadow with the cheers of Zayden's army.

Denita spun slowly, gasping breathless. "We have doubled, my warrior. There are hundreds of fighters together on this hill. I see equal parts Darracians and Quyroos."

He scanned the crowd, clicking his tongue to gage the size of his fighting force, knowing by the noise it had swelled and had more than just the lithe forms of Quyroos. Darracians had joined the ranks. Finally, they were one. The planet was whole, as his father wished. He had fulfilled his destiny. He turned to Denita, holding her by her shoulders. "This is where we part. Stay here." He pulled her close, kissing her full on her lips, leaving her breathless.

"But I am your eyes!" she protested.

"More importantly, you are my heart, and I will keep you safe." He kissed her again and told her. "I will come back for you."

He shouted for his men to follow him, and Denita watched him run forward, knowing he had just told her a lie. Denita followed him stealthily down the hill.

Chapter 26

Like a magnet, V'sair's blue eyes caught and held his uncle's gaze. V'sair stood tall in the water, raising his sword as a beacon for his troops to follow. Their wet skin glistened as though they were covered in diamonds. The army of sickle-shaped spears followed his lead, looking like a sheet of steel. Their feet marched in tandem, the steady thrum of the footsteps echoing off the back wall of the landmass. V'sair's eyes caught the ragtag line of Quyroo and Darracian warriors in readiness on the crest the hills surrounding the Plains of Dawid. He knew at this moment a full brigade of his fighters was making its way from the other shorelines, crushing any opposition. He paused, sucking his breath, a broad smile lighting his face when he realized it was his brother who stood proudly on the ridge. "Brother in arms," he said quietly, then saluted him with is sword. He frowned when there was no return, but the large field became deathly quiet. Restive stallius's whinnied, and V'sair recognized a familiar sound. Hother took that moment to scream wildly, raising herself onto her hind legs to trying to unseat Seren. She pranced toward the water, shaking Seren from her back like an unwanted parasite. He fell onto the red sand hard on his shoulder, watching helplessly as the stallius opened her wings to glide to her beloved master. V'sair reached for her, hugging her muscled neck, inhaling the familiar scent of his mount. Tears prickled the back of his eyelids, but he drew a deep breath, blocking out emotions. He blew gently into her nose, in a fluid motion, pulled himself onto her back, lifting his sword to the heaven, crying out, "For Drakko, for equality, for Darracia!"

A loud cheer deafened the field, marrying the two forces. With a unified war cry, they took off at the same time with the sole purpose of destroying their invaders. The blue tide of fighters raced across the beach toward the incoming gray-and-red mass of warriors descending the hill.

V'sair galloped Hother across the beach, his sword gilded by the suns, Lothen and his black stallius in his line of sight. Sand sprayed behind him, creating a sparkling aura around both V'sair and his stallius. He looked like an avenging spirit, his mount's wings spread in stunning white glory, his face against the creamy coat of the stallius, his white hair entwined with her mane.

Lothen pulled his reins up, making his mount open its wingspan to fly above the bloody fray. V'sair mirrored his movements, and they met, their swords clashing in a tremendous explosion of energy. V'sair's arm shivered from the blow, but he swung around to raise the weapon again for another swipe at his uncle.

They danced in the sky, nicking flesh, hitting bone—equal to the task for defending their territory. Although Lothen had experience, V'sair had agility and youth. V'sair spun to his left, knowing Lothen tried to put him in a position where the suns' dual glare blinded him. V'sair danced Hother in a tight circle. Hother bit the other stallius, making Lothen's animal rear up in anger, frothing at the bit. Lothen held tight, slashing V'sair, opening his forearm wrist to elbow. Blood dripped to leave a trail on the water, falling in tiny ripples on the foaming surface. V'sair stabbed Lothen's thigh, the hiss of pain letting him know he had struck true.

Staf Nuen watched the battle from the listing balcony of the grounded castle. Observing the aerial ballet of Lothen and his nephew V'sair, a smile tugged at his lips. He saw V'sair get in a successful jab at Lothen and whispered, "You should be proud of your son, brother. Tire him, V'sair," he advised to the vacant space. "If you let him exhaust himself, you may yet win." While he was twenty stories up, just this morning the Randam expired, settling the fortress in a muddy lake known for its murky depths. The first two levels sunk below the waterline, the next level filling fast. He felt a presence behind him and turned to see Naje holding her infant.

"You are king, still?" she asked, her face white with worry.

"Does it matter?" He turned back to look at the carnage. The flower of Darracian warriors was gone—people he'd trained with, soldiers with both honor and merit. All that was left was this fighting force of old men and little boys who joined to Zayden and his red troops. "It has all been for nothing."

"What?" Naje stalked to him. "Your son!" She gestured the wrapped infant in her arms.

"Lothen's son. This is no boy of mine. I killed my son with greed and stupidity. Drakko was right."

"What are you talking about?" she demanded. "Is that the graphen talking?"

Staf shook his head. "I wanted to be king because I thought I knew better. I wanted to suppress the Quyroos for all the wrong reason. No species is better than the others. Emmicus was right. The Trivium is whole; one cannot exist without the other."

"You babble. Who is Emmicus?" Naje asked accusingly.

"A very wise man. Darracia cannot stand without the unity of its species." He paused. "I was wrong about everything." He turned his face away.

"That's it?" she shrieked. "That's all you are going to do? I will never forgive you."

He turned to look at her, assessing her coldly. "It's not your forgiveness I am looking for." He turned to stare at the horizon. "I must forgive myself, and I'll never be able to. All is lost," he mumbled. Wearily, he climbed to balance himself upon the balustrade. He looked down into the swirling depths of the lake. "It was all for nothing. I was wrong, all wrong," he said in a shocked whisper. He was so filled with his own sense of rightness he now realized he was empty. There was indeed nothing else. He pitched forward, feeling at peace, allowing himself the last feeling of complete freedom before the water engulfed him, pulling Staf Nuen into obscurity and oblivion.

Naje cursed, watching in helpless horror. She shouted, "Nooooo!" as Staf threw himself out of the fortress. She leaned over, watching his cape spread out like a giant bat, his face staring up, his worry erased. "Old fool," she cursed him. Running from the room, shoving items in a sack. The baby cried, hungry, his pinched, little face blue with rage. She shushed him, rocking against her full breasts until he quieted. "Come, Loki. I will save us. I have always depended upon myself." She kissed the white, downy head, satisfied as her son's eyes slid shut. "It appears that I will continue to do so."

Throwing a dark cape over her head, she raced to the exit, swallowed by the yawning forest outside the castle door.

Chapter 27

The two leaders of the land clashed overhead, their swords ringing in the valley below them. V'sair called out to his Darracian ancestors with the ancient war cry, causing great cheers on the ground below. The battle raged, hand to hand with fierce fighting, leaving a swath of destruction below. Zayden created a line of hiding stationary soldiers on the top of the hill armed with the small slingshots. He led the charge down the incline, stopping his warriors at the base in a coordinated move. Plantan warriors took this as cowardice and moved forward with confidence. Zayden clicked his tongue, gaging the approaching enemy. Then he screamed, "Turn!"

The Quyroos and Darracian soldiers turned to climb up the hill, the Plantans screaming with victory behind them. As they landed on the first terraced area, Zayden's soldiers threw themselves face first on the floor, leaving the oncoming enemy exposed to the line of marksmen above them. Round after round of deadly missiles were loosed, catching the attackers unprepared. The gourds sang as they were loaded then launched in a unending barrage of shrapnel.

Zayden cocked his head, listening as the thud of the rock missiles found their mark on the enemies' torsos. His sonar working, he fielded a blow meant to take off his head by ducking and stabbing his attacker. He paused the noise of the battle receding when he zeroed in on his brother V'sair's war cry. "V'sair." He looked upward, seeing nothing but knowing from the change in the air currents that his brother was flying on Hother above him. He waved, his back unguarded, a target for a Plantan sergeant who stood, taking aim with a gun. He shot at Zayden, the whistling bullet heading toward him. Denita screamed, "Zayden, duck!" Looking around, she spied a pistol in the dead hands of a soldier, took aim, shooting the enemy in the heart.

Zayden dropped to the ground, the bullet tearing at his shoulder, ripping his tunic. He stood, furious, marching while screaming, "Denita. I told you to stay back!"

She ran, throwing herself at him, so they tumbled onto the ground, their legs entangling.

"Why?" She kissed his cheek, filthy with the grime of battle. "Why, my heart? Where you go, I go."

"It's not safe." They rolled into a ravine, the sounds of the fight dying off. "You are female," he said as if that explained everything.

"A female is just as good a fighter as a male, any male, be he Quyroo, Draccian, or Planta!" Denita answered hotly.

Zayden shook his head. "I know. I know. You are right. But, Denita, you are *my* female."

"If you plan of equality, my love, it has to be equality for all," she whispered. "Besides, did you think I could not shoot?"

"I know you can shoot. I have to go back."

This time when he stood to assess the battle, his woman was beside him, protecting his back.

Lothen stared in disbelief as the bulk of his army was cut down by makeshift soldiers without real weapons. V'sair used that moment to rush at him. But Lothen moved, and the stallius took the hit, screaming in pain. The animal spiraled down to the planet, taking Lothen with it. V'sair followed relentlessly.

Lothen's eyes scanned the beach for Seren, for help, angry with his failure to not only hold onto his mount but the ineffectual command of the landed forces. He aimed the dying stallius away from the thick of the fighting, landing with a hard crash. He spied his erstwhile commander, near the waterline on the beach. He was holding onto a girl, a Quyroo, while battling with an older woman. The old Quyroo used a stick against his sword and looked to be tiring. He ducked into the bushes, lost in the confusion on the ground.

V'sair lost Lothen when he landed, his eyes searching the bloody beach. He glanced downward to see a woman used as a shield by Seren. He redirected Hother to move in to help the woman, his mount's hoofs grazing the choppy seas. He landed on the beach, and noticed the fighting had tapered off. Leaping off his stallius, he ran to block Bobbien, saving her from a thrust that would have taken off her head.

"V'sair!" Tulani screamed. "V'sair!"

"You hide behind a woman?" V'sair taunted the Quyroo commander.

"I will kill her before I let you have her again." He backed into the water, holding Tulani, his sword resting on her thin neck.

V'sair could see her pulse beating, the resignation in her eyes. He rushed after them, the water reaching his hips. Seren nicked her, the blood welled to drip into the small swells of the sea. "I will finish the job, V'sair. Come closer. I'd like nothing better!" Seren snarled.

V'sair's breath caught in his throat, as the snout of the giant beast he'd seen under the water arced its vast head above the waterline, its nostrils flaring with the scent of Tulani's blood. It moved its bulky head back and forth, exposing rows of gigantic white teeth. Opening its jaws, it rose from the water, ripping off Seren's head.

"Tulani, jump!" V'sair screamed, propelling him toward her, his hands outreached to grab her. There was the crunch as Seren's head was snapped from his torso and a great sucking sound of the pull from the great fish as it tried to grab Tulani. Tulani floundered, her arms flailing as she slipped in the oily water, slick with the fresh gouts of blood shooting from Seren's corpse. V'sair used his gills, diving deeply, wrapping his arms around her body, placing his mouth over hers to give the breath of life. He felt her go limp in his arms, whether from fear or because she had fainted, but the swells of waves from the furious fish buffeted them both toward the shore line. They emerged—V'sair holding Tulani in his arms—to walk slowly toward the wartorn beach, littered with the dead and dying. The battle was over, he thought with exhaustion, his glassy eyes taking in the carnage. A force of nature plowed into him, wrapping great arms around both V'sair and Tulani.

V'sair looked up to find himself in the crushing embrace of his half brother.

Zayden sniffed the air and said, "You smell like fish, brother." Zayden continued, "and you, Tulani, smell like sunshine."

V'sair took in his brother's weary face, seeing new lines and scars. "Are you hurt?"

"It's a long story, and now is not the time." Zayden smiled. He clicked, getting his bearings. "Sounds like something still going on that way." He pointed to a ridge on the left. "See you after the battle." He dashed off, screaming for his warriors to follow him into the fray. V'sair observed a cocoa-skinned girl devotedly following his brother's moves, covering his back.

V'sair kissed Tulani on her lips. "Have you heard anything from my mother?" he asked hopefully.

Tulani shook her head that she hadn't. Salt crusted her lashes, her eyes were giant pools of shock.

"I will see you later. I know I saw Bobbien. Find her. Get to the castle. I will meet you there," he told her. "Go. I have to finish this." He scanned the beach, looking for Lothen.

Lothen stood on a rock watching the destruction of his army. Holding out his arms, he summoned Geva again. This time the sky darkened, and lightning flashed, stilling the last combatants. Lothen walked out of his hiding place to scream, "Make them pay, Geva!"

Like a plague, Geva swarmed the remaining soldiers, a dark mist descending to choke the life from them. V'sair felt the thickness in the air, the foul evil of Lothen's goddess, despair filling him with dread. He was tired. He had fought and thought victory was in his hands. He watched the black cloud move toward his brother, still fighting high on the final ridge. Slowly it moved, leaving corpses in its wake. V'sair screamed out, "Ozre, Erethe, and Ine, I commend myself to thee.

Great Sradda, what more do you expect from us? After this, you would let them win?" He fell to his knees, his head buried in the pink sand. A great rumble shook him so that he fell over. He heard startled cries as the water in the Hixom Sea boiled, turning the gray water white with foam. An explosion rent the air, and the water parted to reveal a huge volcano rising from the seabed. It roared to life as it got bigger, blotting out the entire horizon. The ground shook with a massive earthquake, the top of the volcano opened, erupting and spewing forth a fierce display of fire. The fighting on the beach ground to a halt, all eyes on the raging inferno that was blazing to massive proportions. V'sair looked up, wonder replacing despair, as multicolored orbs of light raced out of the cone of the volcano. Green, blue, and red orbs flew into the sky, surrounding the dark cloud, reining it in like a net. The black cloud slipped through an opening to move across the large sky. The three orbs raced, getting there before Geva. It was as though they could anticipate her every move. Geva thinned, hoping to escape by dissipating enough she would be too big to contain. The balls of light exploded into a thousand small beams of brightness. They spread out across the sky, filling the horizon, trapping the smoky blackness that was the essence of Lothen's goddess. It struggled against the confines but was no match for the speed and dexterity of the glowing spirals of bright light. They bounced, attacked, and confined Geva, smothering the blackness with light.

Lothen yelled, "Geva!" He watched miserably as the black cloud got smaller, finally disappearing into a small puff of smoke. The orbs turned to him, spinning toward his direction, filling the Plantan king until he was lifted high, his body rigid. He spun in a vortex of color, his white hair burning brightly, until he was dropped into the fuming cone of the volcano, his screams echoing for a full minute afterward. The orbs spread out, pulsing high above the Plains of Dawid, a rainbow of colors reflecting from their depths. The green light bounced forward, taking precedence and sweeping across the land, touching the sand and leaving a lighted path. The lights then gravitated together, forming a single, large ball of green, blue, and red. They floated above the Plains of Dawid like a new sun.

"The Trivium is whole. One is not whole without the other." V'sair stood, intoning the prayer.

Ozre dipped. "The land with grow…"

Ereth's blue light nodded. "Water is life…"

The green in Ine raced again in a great circle around the bowl like structure of the meadow, each revolution making her go faster and faster until all one saw was a shadow of her color. She exploded into dazzling green sparks that filled the space then landed gracefully on the ground.

V'sair walked over to touch the tiny light in his hand. It glowed, pulsing with life. "Ine is the seed," he said in awe.

The large, green orb went back to rest between the others. Her voice became the soft music of a mother's call. "Ine is the seed to make the Desa grow again."

The three orbs bounced to rise above the volcano. All eyes were drawn to a row of ships moving into the atmosphere. They were the Plantan ships used to transport the Darracians to Bina.

V'sair sighed. "Oh, no, not again." He felt his brother behind him.

"Tell me what you see, V'sair."

V'sair turned, realizing his brother was blind. "I'm not sure." He shrugged. "Ships. Another invasion."

Tulani came to his other side. "I told you to find Bobbien and return to the castle."

"I have found Bobbien." V'sair turned to see the old Quyroo behind him, a smile on her face.

"I will never be parted from you again." She took his hand. "We are one, forever, V'sair. In the sky or on the land, we will never be parted again."

Raising her hand, he brushed her bruised knuckles with a kiss.

Zayden mobilized his troops on the ridge, weapons ready. The entire crest was lined with V'sair's Welks, Quyroos, and Darracians standing tall, ready to defend their home. The new volcano smoked lazily from its home in the ocean, filling the sky with the charred odor of fire.

"You should be further back, your highness," Zayden advised his king. "I will meet the enemy on your behalf."

"Only a Grand Mestor can tell me that."

Zayden bowed his head. "I am blind, brother. I am crippled. You will need someone who is not handicapped."

"I need you, brother." V'sair turned to face him, knowing Zayden could sense how important he was to him. "You blindness is a handicap only if you make it one. To me, I see my brother. The only ones I see crippled are the victims who tangled with you. You are the warrior our father expected."

Zayden's eyes misted. "Then as your Grand Mestor, I advise you to remove yourself."

"As your brother only, I respectfully refuse. We meet our destiny together." They turned to face the lead ship, now lowering itself slowly onto the pink soil.

The lead ship's thruster blew the sand in swirling circles as it placed itself onto the pink beach, the doors opening.

A large Darracian stepped out, his eyes scanning the surroundings, his hands wrapped around a baton of sorts as a weapon. Both V'sair and Zayden readied their swords, as the large male turned, holding out his hand to help another from inside the ship. A small boy descended shakily, his head covered with a cowl. He had a decidly feminine grace about his movements. On the last step, the smaller one removed the head covering revealing spiked white hair, and with a gasp, the realization of her identity shocked the crowd. Her worried eyes moved wildly about, coming to rest on her son. "V'sair!" she called, tripping quickly down the ramp.

V'sair dropped his sword, and shouted with joy as he raced to the steps of the ship.

He looked older, bloodied by battle—a warrior king, pride filling her chest.

They met at the bottom of the craft in a loving embrace. It was so silent; only the wind made noise.

V'sair was shocked at her fragility as well as surprised by the possessive glare of the draconian Darracian assisting her down.

"It is over, Mo'mo. Darracian is whole." He assured her.

Reminda looked to the clouds seeing only sky, not a building on the horizon. Syos was gone.

"Dado's dream has come true. All Darracians are equal, be they called Quyroo or Welk, no one will live above or below. They will share in the bounty of the land equally."

"The Elements have spoken." Bobbien came forward to embrace her friend. "The Elements have made it so."

Epilogue

Tulani and V'sair were both crowned and married in a beautiful celebration. They rebuilt the royal city on the Plains of Dawid. Land, sea, and air lived together in harmony. It was an age of growth. The arts flourished, and Darracia became an epicenter of culture for the galaxy. V'sair and Tulani were sought out to help with other planets, advising them how to end disputes. Their family grew, and with the first child born just a year later, the succession assured. Cawa was beautiful and smart, the perfect heir for her parents. Zayden's sight never came back. As the respected Grand Mestor and the father of a growing brood, it made no difference. Denita worked to find ways to compensate him, winning the Galacial Prize for Health and Science and was celebrated all over the Galaxy. They had six sons, each as different and diverse as the solar system. From the army to medicine, each one embraced a profession that brought grace and honor to the family. Reminda lived in a compound not far from all her grandchildren. She had a noted salon that people longed to join to sit at her table and discuss how to make society better. She championed prisoners everywhere, working hard to find solutions to punishments that were more humane. Marek never left her side, and once V'sair got used to his presence, they found that second chances are the sweet aperitif to life. There was peace and prosperity in the land, even in the Deep Fells where a young, blue-skinned boy climbed among the trees in the new forest, growing along side the seedlings of peace.

Other books by Michael

Brood X: A Firsthand Account of the Great Cicada Invasion

Stillwell: A Haunting on Long Island

The Hanging Tree: A Novella

About the Author

Born and raised on Long Island, Michael has always had a fascination with horror writing and found-footage films. He wanted to incorporate both with his debut novel, *Brood X*. After earning a degree in English and an MBA, he worked various jobs before settling into being a full-time author. He currently resides on Long Island with his wife and children.

michaelphillipcash@gmail.com

Made in the USA
Columbia, SC
19 November 2017